About this book

Michael Lawrence uses a lot of his own experiences and observations in the Jiggy McCue stories. Like missing a plane to Disneyland Paris, coming across a Punch and Judy booth that lacked a Mr Punch, and trying to get out of a locked holiday flat with cutlery while a carnival was going on. All three of these incidents occur early on in this book, in which Jiggy, Pete and Angie go on holiday with their parents and meet an old adversary.

If you've read *The Killer Underpants* you'll recognise the name Neville the Devil at once. If you haven't, you can meet him here for the first time and read about the Musketeers' original encounter with him another day. The Jiggy books can be read in any order, but to get the most out of them (Jiggy & Co are a wee bit older in each one) we suggest that you read them in the order in which they were written, which is:

The Poltergoose, The Killer Underpants
The Toilet of Doom, Maggot Pie
The Snottle, Nudie Dudie
Neville the Devil

ONE FOR ALL AND ALL FOR LUNCH!
Visit Michael at his website: www.wordybug.com

ORCHARD BOOKS
96 Leonard Street, London EC2A 4XD
Orchard Books Australia
32/45-51 Huntley Street, Alexandria, NSW 2015
1 84362 879 1
A Paperback Original
First published in Great Britain in 2005
Text © Michael Lawrence 2005
Illustrations © Ellis Nadler 2005
The rights of Michael Lawrence to be identified as the author
and of Ellis Nadler to be identified as the illustrator
of this work have been asserted by them in accordance with
the Copyrights, Designs and Patents Act, 1988.
A CIP catalogue record for this book is available from the British Library
5 7 9 10 8 6
Printed in Great Britain

A JIGGY McCUE STORY

Michael Lawrence

ORCHARD BOOKS

*This book is dedicated to
You, dear reader!
From little me*

Chapter one

We were just pulling in to a motorway service station for a widdle-and-fodder break when I had this sudden feeling we were in for a bad time. There were seven of us in two cars, Mum and Dad and me in one, Pete and Angie and his dad (Oliver) and her mum (Audrey) in the other. The dads were driving. My mother says dads like to drive because the car is the only place they can feel in charge. When we pulled in, I rushed over to Pete and Angie and told them about my sudden feeling.

'You always have a feeling we're in for a bad time,' Angie said cheerfully.

'Not this sudden,' I said.

She pushed past me. 'Well this time you're wrong.'

'I wouldn't be so sure about that,' I said to her back.

She spun round, still cheerful. 'One more word,' she said, 'and I stick your head in the nearest litter bin. That'll be your bad time.'

'Relax, Jig,' said Pete, also cheerful. 'Nothing bad's going to happen. Not this time. I feel it in my armpits.'

I sighed. Maybe they were right. Maybe I was worrying about nothing. I dumped the nervous frown and switched back to Cheerful Mode. Berk. I should learn to trust my bad feelings. Specially the sudden ones.

I'd better tell you why we were so damn cheerful. We were going on our summer hols. Yep. And not just anywhere this time. This time we were going Abroad. I'd never been Abroad. Nor had Pete and Angie. Best of all, we were going by plane. We'd never been in a plane before either. We had this ten o'clock flight to catch, that's ten in the morning, and we had to check in at the airport two hours before takeoff, which had meant getting up with the birdies. Our big shiny plane would fly us over water and some land to JoyWorld. You've probably heard of JoyWorld. Amusement park the size of a small country, with hotels and lakes and all sorts of rides. We were going to stay in one of the hotels and walk round the lakes and go on things we hadn't even imagined yet. Some of the things we hadn't even imagined yet would swoop right up into the sky before crashing right down into the ground and give us the galloping hysterics just before we tottered off to throw up over a parent. We were really looking forward to that.

Like I said, there were seven of us, including the four Golden Oldies. I thought there should have been eight. Stallone had never been Abroad either, or in a plane. Stallone's our cat. But Mum said that if we took him out of the country he might have to go into quarantine when we brought him back and we wouldn't see him for ages. 'Let's take him with us,' said Dad, who's not a huge Stallone fan. We didn't of course. We left his bowl with Janet Overton next door. Stallone's, I mean, not Dad's. Stallone always goes where his bowl is. One of Stallone's favourite pastimes, bowling.

But I'm going to tell you something now, and I want you to pay attention. Are you listening? Right. Here it is. Do not, whatever you do, go on holiday with parents. Any parents. In fact, any adults. Ban them. Leave them at home handcuffed to freezers. Take them with you at your peril. You can let them pay for the tickets and all the rest, that's

OK. You can let them organise everything, and give you a big fat wad of the folding stuff, or better still a credit card with your name on it, but never ever let them go with you. When they're not yelling at you, or smoothing your hair, or making plans for you to visit model villages, they're embarrassing you in public places. My mother is especially good at this.

'JIGGY!' she bawled at the motorway widdle-and-fodder joint, so loudly that every head for miles turned to stare at me coming out of the Gents. 'DID YOU WASH YOUR HANDS AFTER GOING TO THE TOILET?!'

It's parents that should be put in quarantine. Permanently.

It was as I was exiting the Gents and my mother was screeching that something unexpected happened. A big stripy beach ball bounced out of nowhere – bounce, bounce, bounce – and stopped dead at my feet so I had to jump over it. When I jumped I flung my arms out to save myself. They closed around a two-metre-high plastic rabbit with a weight problem and tombstones for teeth. The Big Fat Bunny wobbled and started to fall forward. I held on, I don't know why. And over we went. It was a slow fall. You know, one of those slo-mo moves you see in action films. When my back finally smacked the ground, Big Fat Bunny was on top of me. He was heavy enough for me to feel kind of flat about things, but not so heavy that it stopped my ears working. I mention this because my ears heard this rattle-rattle-clink-clink sound all around. But then I noticed two Big Fat Bunny eyes staring into mine and stopped harking to rattle-rattle-clink-clink-type sounds. Up close those eyes were terrifying.

The BFB and I stopped staring into one another's eyes when security men hauled him off and jerked me to my feet. It was then that I realised what all the rattle-rattle-clink-clinking had been about. It had been about a million coins hitting the floor and rolling around looking for holes to drop though. These were the coins that had been put in the slot in Big Fat Bunny's plastic chest only to shoot out of a flap in its bunniferous bott when it flattened me. People were scrabbling like maniacs for the coins. Even Pete was on his knees filling his pockets until Angie grabbed his collar and lifted him into a twitching crouch.

And then my parents were there, and my mother was apologising humbly to the security men – apologising for me, her terrible son – and Dad was saying 'Well done, Jig,' with a smirk. When the Big Fat Bunny was upright again a few of the coin collectors came over guilty and formed an orderly queue to drop the coins back in his chest slot. I ducked under some arms and between some legs and scurried to the food counters to give people a chance to talk about me behind my back. Angie was just two steps behind.

'What happened there?' she asked at the first food counter.

'The Big Fat Bunny fell on me,' I said.

'You must have nudged it.'

'I didn't nudge it. I threw my arms round it.'

'What did you do that for? Love at first sight?'

'I was jumping over a ball. Grabbed the BFB to save myself.'

'What ball?'

'That ball.'

A young kid had caught up with the ball and was walking away with it held to his chest, a happy grin separating his cheeks. I wanted to shout,

'There's the culprit! Stare at him, not me!' But I didn't. I said: 'Great. Hash browns.'

I was struggling to pick up a hash brown with the big tweezers provided when Pete shunted up.

'It's not fair,' he said. 'Dad told me to put the money back.'

'I hope you did,' Angie said.

'I gave it to him to put back. Most of it.'

'You mean you kept some?'

Pete tapped his pocket. 'The odd bit and piece.'

'Peter Garrett,' she said, 'that is charity money.'

'I'm a charity, didn't I mention that?'

'Go and give the rest to your dad.'

'Why should I?'

She pasted her nose to his. 'Because I'm telling you to.'

Pete knows better than to argue with Angie Mint when she's nosing him. He shuffled off, grumbling.

It hadn't been easy, but I'd managed to tweezer three hash browns on to my plate by this time. Beans next. I dipped the giant spoon in the baked bean bucket.

'That must have been your sudden bad feeling,'

Angie said, examining wrappers for E-additives. 'That a charity bunny was gonna pulp you.'

'No, that wasn't it,' I said.

'It wasn't?'

'No. Don't think so.'

'You think the sudden bad feeling was for something that hasn't happened yet?' I nodded. 'What?'

I shrugged. 'Dunno.'

'Jiggy, we're heading for an airport.'

'I know.'

'And a plane.'

'I know.'

'Which will fly up into the air.'

'I know.'

'With us in it.'

'I know.'

'Maybe we should mention your bad feeling,' she said.

'I know. I mean who to?'

'The Golden Oldies, who else?'

'Tell our parents I had a sudden bad feeling as we're about to get on a plane?' I said. 'I don't think so.'

She grabbed a bundle of E-additives and we left it at that. Something was going to happen, something bad, but we couldn't tell a soul. We would just have to see if we survived. Or not.

Chapter Two

Angie jumped cars for the second half of the journey. She did this because she was sick of sitting next to Pete. No one should be forced to sit with Pete for more than ten minutes. I know that better than anyone because I sit with him in class for hours every day. We're not supposed to talk in class, but you have to do something to take your mind off being there, which means I get quite a lot of earfuls of Garrett and his stupid jokes. I get into trouble all the time for just telling him to shut up. Teachers have no idea what it's like to be a kid. Specially a kid sitting next to Pete Garrett.

We were already running a bit late because Dad had hit a winning streak on the fruit machines at the service station. Oliver, Pete's dad, hadn't been in much of a hurry either, though he wasn't doing so well on the machine next door. We might not have left when we did if the mums hadn't nagged so much. That bit of lateness was bad enough, but three miles short of the airport we ran into slow-moving traffic.

'We'll never make it now,' Mum said, biting her nails.

'We'll make it,' said Dad. But he didn't sound too sure.

The traffic thinned out around the time the airport car park signs appeared. There were four car parks and we followed the sign for Car Park Three, which seemed a pretty good idea seeing as that was the one we were booked into. But at Car Park Three we found that our spaces, B87 and B88, had cars in them already. Parked cars. Dad and Oliver squealed to a halt beside a little blue hut where the man who ran the car park lived. They jumped out and stormed to the little blue window.

'Those spaces are booked for a week,' the man in the window said when they told him what was up.

'We know,' said Oliver. 'We booked them.'

The man asked what names the spaces had been booked in and checked his computer screen. 'Hanker and Wok,' he said.

'What?' said Dad and Oliver together.

'Wok. And Hanker. Not your names. Let's see your tickets.'

They marched to the cars for the tickets, which the women handed them. Then they marched back to the little hut. The man looked at the tickets.

'Wrong car park.'

'What?' said Dad and Ollie again. They were really getting the hang of that word.

'This is Car Park Four. You want Three. Go back to the last roundabout and this time follow the sign to Car Park Three.'

'We did follow the sign to Car Park Three,' Dad said. 'It pointed here.'

'Is that a fact?'

'Yes, it's a fact.'

'I have a thought,' the man said.

The dads leaned forward, keen to hear it.

'What I'm thinking,' the man said, 'is that when you get home after your holiday you go to an optician for two pairs of specs. Then you'll see the sign clearer next time.'

Dad and Oliver snarled, jumped back in the cars, and burnt rubber through the exit. And back at the roundabout? We all saw it, plain as day, the sign for Car Park Three pointing another way entirely.

'I swear…' said Dad.

'That won't help,' said Mum. 'We're cutting it really fine now.'

'I know.'

'Even with this mistake, even with the slow traffic, we wouldn't have been this pushed if some of us hadn't wasted so much time at that service station.'

'Yeah, Jig.' Dad glanced over his shoulder. 'You and the charity rabbit.'

'I don't mean him,' Mum said. 'I mean you and those rotten fruit machines.'

'I was winning!' Dad said, banging his foot down so hard our heads nearly came off.

Spaces B87 and B88 in the real Car Park Three were waiting for us, as empty and lonely as they should have been until we screeched into them. Everyone jumped out, bags were hauled, and we ran with them to the bus stop by the gate to catch the bus that was going to take us to the airport just in time to catch the plane. Except…

No bus.

'Now what?' said Oliver.

'Buses every five minutes,' said Audrey Mint,

pointing to a notice which said that.

'You don't want to believe everything you read,' Dad said.

Oliver agreed. 'Remember the sign for Car Park Three.'

'We were wrong about that, that's all,' said Mum.

'Ha!' said Dad and Oll in perfect sync. They were like a double act today.

'We should be in our seats on the plane by now,' said Audrey.

'Relax,' said Oliver. 'They always allow extra time for late arrivals.'

When Dad backed him up on this, Mum and Audrey rolled their eyes. Pete and Angie and I said nothing. We've learnt over the years that when the Golden Oldies are stressed to make like wallpaper. That way we don't get picked on for absolutely nothing.

The little blue airport bus pulled in two minutes twenty-four seconds later. I timed it. The driver got down like he had all the time in the world and lobbed our bags into the belly of the bus. We got on in a hurry, like it would leave without us if we didn't, with or without the driver.

'You're leaving now, right?' Oliver said when the driver heaved himself slowly up into his seat.

'Couple minutes,' he said, opening *The Daily Buttock*.

'But our plane's about to take off!' said Audrey.

'Timetable,' said the driver.

'But we're the only passengers, what does it matter?' Dad said.

'Buses depart every five minutes. There's the notice.'

We sat rigid in our seats counting out the final two minutes.

'Time!' Oliver yelled on the dot.

The driver put his paper down, blew his nose, checked his eyebrows in the rear-view mirror, and drove slowly towards the exit.

'Can't you get a move on?' Dad said.

'Fifteen-mile-an-hour limit here,' the driver replied.

'Could've got there faster on a one-wheeled skateboard,' Pete whispered to us. Ange and I shook our heads at him. A warning to make like he didn't exist. If we'd known what was to come we might not have done that.

Now we come to the proof that my bad feelings should be paid attention to. I could go into a lot of detail about this, really spin it out, make a big thing of it, but that would bore you and it would bore me, so I'll give you the short version. By the time we got to the airport...

Our plane had gone!

'Bet you're feeling pretty pleased with yourself now,' Angie said to me when we'd got over the shock.

'Why would I be feeling pleased with myself?'

'Your sudden bad feeling.'

'I'd rather have caught the plane,' I said.

Pete didn't say a word about my sudden bad feeling or missing the plane. He just came and stood in front of me and screwed his face up like I'd made it happen, then kicked a suitcase. He got an earful for that from the next person in the queue, whose case it was.

'There must be other planes to JoyWorld,' said Audrey. 'It's a major holiday destination after all.'

'You can't just hop on another plane like it was the next bus,' Dad said.

'Well suppose Aud and I go and see,' Mum said.

'Yes, let's,' said Audrey. 'Better than standing round here.'

'Wasting your time,' said Oliver. 'The whole world wants to catch a plane at this time of year.'

They went anyway. They were gone quite a while. It was a while filled with faint hope. Mums are good at sorting stuff, we all knew that. We stood there, the five of us, waiting with the faint hope, tapping our feet to the Salvation Airforce band under the clock. Our spirits lifted when we saw the mothers shimmying back through the crowds queuing happily for planes that wouldn't leave without them.

Until we saw their faces.

'Not one empty seat for love or money,' said Mum.

'On a single airline,' said Audrey.

'Holiday time,' said Oliver. 'I told you.'

'Question is, what do we do now?' said Mum.

'Only one thing we can do,' said Dad.

'Turn round and go back home,' said Ollie.

Audrey's eyes looked like they were going to melt. 'I was so looking forward to this holiday,' she said.

'So was I,' said Mum, close to the waterworks herself.

Even Angie was a bit mushy in the peeper area. 'I don't want to go home. I'm sick of home. I want a break from home.'

We all did, even Dad and Oll, who hadn't really wanted to go to JoyWorld. So there we stood with all our baggage, tapping our feet to the Salvation Airforce band under the clock, while millions swept round us with cases on wheels, passports and tickets in hands, heading for signs marked Departures.

'Excuse me,' a voice said. 'I couldn't help overhearing...'

Seven heads turned. Fourteen eyes stared at a chest. Then they lifted to look at the face fronting the head stuck on the neck above the chest. Not that you could see much of the face. It was hairier than a bear's behind, but grey. Little round glasses on the end of a nose like a beak. All he needed was a pointy hat and a dressing gown covered in stars and he'd have looked like an asylum-seeker from Hogwarts.

'Yes?'

'You appear to be a trifle short of a holiday destination.'

28

'You could say that,' Mum said, glaring at Dad.

'Well I know it's not the same as JoyWorld,' the tall hairy geezer said, 'but if it's of any interest I know of a holiday flat at Wonkton-on-Sea that's vacant for the week.'

'How did he know we were going to JoyWorld?' I said to Pete and Angie.

'He overheard,' Angie said.

'Nobody's mentioned JoyWorld for at least ten minutes.'

'So he's been overhearing for ten minutes, what does it matter?'

'Sounds dodgy to me,' said Pete.

'Everything sounds dodgy to you,' I said.

'It usually is,' he muttered.

We stood tapping our feet to the Salvation Airforce band under the clock while the tall hairy geezer told our parents about the empty holiday flat on the coast.

'If not for this last-minute thing that's cropped up,' he said, 'I'd be there myself now. Do you know Wonkton? Nice resort. Not too commercial. The flat overlooks the town. But it's up to you...'

'Oh, we couldn't,' said Mum. 'Could we?' she said to Aud.

'Well it's something,' said Aud.

'It's going begging,' said the tall hairy geezer.

'Rent free, you say?' said Dad.

'All paid for.'

'But is it big enough for seven?' Mum asked.

'Oh, I think so. The children might be a mite cramped, but I'm sure they'll manage.'

We swapped fed-up glances. Of course we'd manage being cramped. We were just kids.

Quick whispered conflab between the Golden Oldies.

'What do you think?'

'It has to be better than going home.'

'We don't know what the place is like.'

'We know what home's like.'

'Well I say we accept.'

'So do I. Sounds like fate to me.'

It wasn't fate. Fate had nothing to do with it. But it would be twenty-four hours before we realised that. We kids, I mean. The GOs never did find out. The lanky beardy type held up a set of keys. My mother took the keys and made a note of the address and how to get there, and the man glided off like his sandals were on wheels. Suddenly some of us were all smiles again.

'Well this is a turn-up for the book, isn't it?' Mum said.

'A flat in this country?' I said. 'Oh yeah, terrific.'

'Beggars can't be choosers,' she said.

'We weren't begging.'

'Rather go home, would you, Jiggy?'

'No, course I wouldn't rather go home, but – '

'Well let's be off then.'

Everyone turned around and lugged cases and bags towards the exit. Pete, Angie and I trailed behind.

'Rather it was JoyWorld,' one of us said.

'Me too,' said another of us.

'And me,' said a third of us.

'Well at least we won't have to listen to that rotten band any more,' said I.

'What rotten band?' said Pete and Angie.

We followed the Golden Oldies through the swishy doors to the bus stop, where we arranged our luggage around us again and stood waiting for another little blue bus to take us back to Car Park Three.

'We'll claim the parking back,' Dad said.

'Not just the parking,' said Oliver. 'Full refund of the air fare.'

'Think they'll cough up?'

'If they don't they'll see me in court.'

The mothers sighed. Not hard to read their minds. 'Macho twits,' they were thinking. I agreed with them. If I get like that when I'm old Angie has instructions to drop me off something high, like a crane. Or a giraffe.

Chapter Three

The drive to Wonkton-on-Sea took about an hour and a half. Every now and then on the way Ange and I swapped unhappy expressions that said that if we hadn't missed the plane we'd be dancing round JoyWorld with big fat grins on our faces any time now.

But when we drove into Wonkton we saw something that made us forget JoyWorld for a while. It was Wonkton Carnival Day, and everywhere you looked there were fancy floats, jugglers on stilts, clowns, all sorts of things, and crowds lining the streets and cheering. It was so loud and hooty, with trumpets and drums and singing and all that you couldn't have heard a bomb go off.

Mum looked back at us and smiled.

'Looks like fun!' she shouted above the racket.

'Fun!' shouted Dad, not smiling.

Sensible people would have waited for the

carnival to go by, but our drivers, Melvin McCue and Oliver Garrett, had no plans to stop till we reached our new destination. They couldn't drive fast, though, because the moment we hit the main street an army of carnival types swarmed around us and between us. Ours was the car in front and we soon lost sight of the others in theirs. Dad got less happy by the minute. He wasn't amused when one insane face after another flattened its nose against our windows and made us jump, and when a geek in spangles and green tights rolled across the bonnet he stuck his head out and told him to get off or become a bad memory. The spangly bonnet-roller chortled, threw his patchwork hat in the air, and leapfrogged over some shoulders.

Mum had the directions to the flat, so she was the one telling Dad which way to go. She needn't have bothered, because the carny route seemed to be the same as ours, up a very steep hill. Steep hills at slow speeds in our car worry my father, but we just about made it to the top, probably because there were so many people behind us, also trying to get up. On top of the hill there was this tall brown building which Mum said must be the one we wanted.

'Why must it be the one we want?!' Dad shouted over the noise.

'Because the name on the plaque is the same as the name on this piece of paper!' Mum shouted back.

'The name on the what?!'

'The plaque!'

'What plaque?!'

'That plaque!'

The name of our holiday home was Journey's End.

'How's the Bad Feeling coming?!' Angie shouted in my lug.

'Just took a nose-dive!' I shouted in hers.

A black arrow painted on the wall pointed to an archway. When Dad drove through the archway we half expected the carnival to follow us, but it didn't. In the little car park on the other side of the arch Mum leapt out and started heaving luggage out of the boot. Not everything. My mother packs for armies. By the time Dad and Ange and I were out, Mum was already opening the door of Journey's End with one of the keys the lofty hippie had given her. Angie grabbed one of the debooted bags, which meant I had to as well. Dad chose a pair of shoes. Two of us went in. All four of us might have gone in, but there wasn't room to swing Stallone in there. It was just a hallway with some stairs going up. Dad complained that the place smelt of boiled cabbage and Mum said, 'Nothing's ever good enough for you, is it?'

'JoyWorld might have been,' he said. 'Cost enough. Money down the pan.'

The staircase was narrow and the bags weren't, so it felt like quite a climb. About halfway up there was little platform sort of thing and a door, but Mum said it wasn't our door. The hairy hippy had told us that our flat was Flat 1 and this door had Flat 2 on it, so we kept going. At the top Mum opened the door of Flat 2 with the other key. We followed her in. The flat wasn't bad. Not great, but not bad. Three bedrooms, living room, bathroom, kitchen, empty birdcage. I went to the big picture window. You could see right down into the town from there. I looked for the other car. No sign of it in the swirling carnival below. I saw something else from that window, though. A distant patch of glistening sea between buildings and trees. I liked that little bit of sea.

Mum was going round flinging the other windows open to let air in because it was hot in there. Dad asked her to put the kettle on because he was gasping.

'Why don't you?' she said.

'I've been driving.'

'And that's it, is it? End of effort? Feet up all the way from now on?'

'If I can get away with it,' he said.

Mum went to the kitchen and ran the tap for a while because she didn't trust the water. It's sad when you can't even trust water, don't you think? When she was satisfied she filled the kettle and plugged it in. But then she realised. She'd packed tea bags, thinking we were going abroad, but they were still in the car, in another case. She told Dad to go and get it. Dad pulled a sour face and went to the door, which had closed because it was on one of those powerful safety-hinge things that crush old ladies.

'It's stuck,' he said.

'What's stuck?' Mum said.

'The door.'

'Try turning the handle.'

'I am turning the handle.'

'Here, let me.'

She elbowed him in the ribs and turned the handle. The door didn't budge. It seemed to have locked itself when it closed, and there was no keyhole this side.

'Now what?' Dad said.

'Try a library card,' said Mum.

'I haven't got a library card.'

'I was being sarcastic. If you had a library card you'd probably read books. If you read books there's an outside chance you'd know how to open a door.'

'OK, Brainiac,' Dad said. 'You tell me how to open a door from the inside without a key.'

'Or a keyhole,' I said. Risky, speaking up at moments like that, but they ignored me anyway.

Mum handed Dad a credit card. He said credit cards only worked in films and she said, 'Try it anyway,' and he did. It didn't work.

'This reminds me of the winter day we couldn't get into the car because the locks were frozen,' Mum said, mainly to Angie who hadn't heard this. 'He'd left the lock-defrost spray in the car and there was only one other way to thaw the ice. He peed on the lock.'

Angie giggled. 'Did it work?'

'Better than the stuff in the can. Pity this lock's not frozen.'

Dad tried several other things, including a drinking straw found in a kitchen cupboard, the sharp end of a feather from the window sill, and cutlery. Yes, my father tried to open the door of our rent-free holiday flat with a straw, a feather, a knife, a fork and a spoon. Nothing worked.

'I need a wee,' Angie said, heading for the bathroom.

'Must be the thought of the personal lock-defroster,' I said.

Mum came out of the bedroom she'd decided would be hers and Dad's. 'No answer,' she said. She was holding his mobile. She often uses his because it costs her less.

'Answer?' Dad said, sliding his favourite Help the Aged comb down the side of the lock.

'From Audrey. Just her message service. Must have forgotten to switch her phone on.'

'Try Ollie.'

'Already have. Same result. He probably forgot to charge his battery. He hardly ever remembers. Like you. Must be a male thing.'

Dad shoved the comb further in. 'My phone's always charged.'

'Yes, because I charge it.'

Dad swore. The comb had snapped.

'Mel!' Mum said sharply.

'What?'

'I've asked you not to say that word in front of Jiggy.'

'What's wrong with "what"?' Dad said.

'Not "what". The other word.'

'What other word?'

'The swear word.'

'What swear word?'

'The swear word you used when your rotten comb snapped.'

'I was very fond of that comb.'

'Fond or not, don't use that word in front of him please.'

'I don't even know what I said. What was it?'

Mum mouthed the word at him.

'Eh?' he said.

She mouthed it again, slowly, stretching her lips in all directions.

'No, still don't get it. You, Jiggy?'

'Yeah, I got it.'

'What was it?'

I told him.

'Jiggy!' Mum said. 'I don't want to hear you using that word.'

'You used it.'

'I was only repeating what your father said.'

'Well don't,' I said. 'You're a bad influence on your son.'

I sloped into the living room. Neat exit, I thought.

Because the windows were open the carnival was almost as noisy up here as it was in the streets below. When Angie came out of the bathroom we stood at the main window looking down at the thousands of people in colourful costumes, the fantastic floats and all.

'Wouldn't mind going down there now we've arrived,' she said.

'Me neither,' I said. 'If we weren't prisoners.'

We watched the carnival for a while, then looked

at the bright little wedge of water between the buildings and trees.

'No sea at JoyWorld,' I said.

'No. I was looking forward to JoyWorld, though.'

'So was I. But there's no sea there.'

'Nobody said there was.'

'No, but there's sea here, so it could be worse.'

'Who are you trying to convince?' she said.

'Me.'

Suddenly we heard Dad shouting. Couldn't make out what he was saying but he sounded like he was in the kitchen now. We went out to the hall. From there we could see into two of the bedrooms. Mum was in the best one, putting a couple of things on hangers so that when Aud and Ollie arrived they'd know whose room it was.

'What's Dad yelling for?'

Mum shrugged. 'If it wasn't one thing it'd be another.'

He was hanging out of the kitchen window, bellowing down at someone in the crowd below.

'I SAID WE'RE LOCKED IN!'

We looked over his shoulders. A policeman on

the pavement was trying to hear him through all the happy shouting and music. We saw his mouth open but couldn't hear what he said, which probably meant he hadn't heard Dad either. He was waving his arms about in sign language which said, 'Yep. Bet it looks good from up there.'

'WE CAN'T GET OUT!' Dad screamed.

'Best we've ever had,' the copper answered silently. 'On holiday, are you?'

'BLITHERING IDIOT!' Dad roared.

'Couldn't agree more,' mouthed the man in blue.

'JIG, GET ME SOME...' he dropped his voice, mainly because I was nine centimetres from it. 'Get me a piece of paper.'

'Where would I get a piece of paper from?' I asked.

'Well I don't know, just get some. I want to drop a note down to Mr Plod but I daren't leave the window or I could lose him.'

'Some paper in the bathroom,' Angie said.

'Great.'

While she was gone, Dad carried on shouting at the happy police chappie, who went right on not understanding.

'Here,' said Angie, handing him the pink toilet roll.

'Couple of sheets would have done,' he said.

'Couple of sheets might flutter away between here and the ground,' Angie said.

'Good point.'

Mum also joined us now. 'What's going on?' she said.

'Dad's trying to talk to this policeman.'

'Policeman?'

'Yes, he's — '

I was interrupted by my father shouting something unkind at the copper to keep his attention while he — Dad — printed the words 'HELP! WE'RE LOCKED IN! RELEASE US!' Then he dropped the toilet roll. The copper saw it coming and stepped aside, laughing. This wasn't the first jolly T-roll he'd had thrown at him today, you could tell.

'READ IT, YOU RAVING PLONKER!' Dad shrieked.

The toilet roll, unravelling all the way down, had bounced off a big rubber mouse with a kid sitting in it, and ended up around the feathery headdress of Sitting Bull or Standing Chicken or whoever he was supposed to be. But luck was with us, just this once, because the first two sheets, the ones Dad had written on, fluttered in front of the copper's eyes. He read the words and looked up at us again. This time Dad didn't shout. This time he nodded like his head was trying to take a weekend break from his neck. The cop got the message. He shot through the archway, up the stairs, and a minute later he was outside the flat, knocking.

'What does he expect us to do? Dad said. 'Open the door?'

'ARE YOU REALLY LOCKED IN?!' the copper shouted.

'YES!' Dad shouted back. 'WE REALLY ARE LOCKED IN!'

'WELL HAVEN'T YOU GOT A KEY?!'

'YES, WE HAVE A KEY, BUT IT'S A SAFETY LOCK AND THERE'S NO KEYHOLE THIS SIDE. SAFETY LOCK! HA! THAT'S A JOKE!'

'THIS IS A JOKE?' hollered the rozzer.

My mother pulled Dad aside and put her mouth to the door.

'NO! IT'S NOT A JOKE! REPEAT. NO JOKE! THE

KEY WON'T WORK FROM THE INSIDE! WE'RE STUCK IN HERE!'

'WELL, WHAT DO YOU WANT ME TO DO ABOUT IT?' the copper yelled back.

'YOU'RE THE POLICE!' Mum bawled. 'WHAT DO YOU SUGGEST?!'

'I'M NOT THE POLICE!'

'YOU'RE NOT THE POLICE?'

'NO, I'M PART OF THE CARNIVAL! ENJOY YOURSELVES!'

Then there was silence. Silence in the flat anyway. It wasn't a very long one. My mother pulled herself together, said something unpleasant and flew into the kitchen. I followed her. So did Angie. Dad didn't bother. Mum turned the cold tap full on, half filled the plastic washing-up bowl, and carried it to the window. We went with her. Looked down with her. Saw the carnival cop come out into the street. Mum shouted at him.

'HEY, YOU!'

I don't know how he heard her in all the noise – maybe it's my mother's screech – but he looked up, and as he looked up Mum tipped the washing-up bowl and drenched him from helmet to

clod-hoppers. 'THANKS FOR THE ASSISTANCE!'
she shrieked.

This time the fake copper only replied in
sign language.

Chapter Four

It was just as well that Audrey eventually turned her phone on and called Dad on his. Well, she called Mum first, but Mum hadn't turned hers on, which gave Dad a chance to be sarky. Mum told Aud and Oliver how to get to the flat, and when they finally managed to mow a path through the crowds and park in the courtyard they came upstairs. Not much point really, coming upstairs, because we had the only key (and no, it wouldn't fit under the door, we tried) but at least we could shout at one another through the wood. Dad suggested throwing the key down to them in the street.

'Not a good idea,' Mum said.

'Why not?'

'There's a drain right below the kitchen window.'

'So we don't use the kitchen window,' Dad said.

'It's the only one that overlooks the street.'

'So we avoid the drain.'

'There'll be a breeze.'

'A breeze?'

'Or something. Always is. You throw a key down and if there's a drain within four or five yards the key goes down it. If there's no breeze to nudge it, then the person you throw it to will fumble it, or it'll bounce off their shoulder, and then we all watch the key go down the drain. It's a nine times out of ten thing.'

'Are you still there?' Oliver shouted through the door.

'No, we just popped out for a beer!' Dad shouted back. He wasn't in a great mood. Probably the broken comb. He'd have to use Mum's now, which had teeth like a combine harvester. He'd be bald by the end of the week.

'HAVE YOU TRIED A CREDIT CARD IN THE LOCK?' Audrey bawled.

'YES!' Mum bawled back. 'DIDN'T WORK!'

It was Angie who thought of tying the key to a long piece of string and lowering it out of the window to waiting hands below.

'That would be a really good idea,' Dad said, 'if we had a long piece of string.'

'There might be some in one of the kitchen drawers,' Mum said. She went to look. Came back.

'Nope.'

'We could knot some sheets together,' I said.

'Too thick,' said Dad.

'So we tear them to ribbons.'

'They're not our sheets,' said Mum.

'Who cares? This is an emergency.'

'We could put the key in the pocket of a pair of jeans or trousers and lower them,' Angie suggested.

'Lower them with what?' I asked.

'Other clothes. We knot them together by the arms or legs, with the jeans or trousers at the bottom.'

'Another good idea,' Dad said, 'if someone −' (he glared at Mum) '− hadn't left the case with most of the clothes in down in the car.'

'We do have some clothes up here,' Angie said.

'Only a couple of things on hangers in the bedroom,' Mum said.

'I mean the ones we're wearing.'

We looked each other up and down.

'I don't think so,' I said.

'Have you got any better ideas?' Mum said.

'No, but...'

'OK, so come on.'

'No, wait,' I said.

'Strip!' she commanded.

Five minutes later we were down to our undies and I was wishing I was wearing anything but what I had on down below.

'Where...' Mum said, and tried again. 'Where did you get that?'

'From the market in town,' I said.

'And you thought you'd wear it to go away in?'

'Seemed like a fun idea at the time.'

I'd better tell you what it was. It was a jockstrap. A shiny black leatherette jockstrap, with nothing – like nothing – behind. Down the front, in a sort of column, were these letters.

Y
O
U
N
G
M
A
N

When the light hit the letters, like it did when I dropped my jeans, they started flashing in different colours, one after the other.

'You get too much pocket money,' Dad said.

We knotted everything except our undies together and Dad threw the result out of the kitchen window, cleverly remembering to keep hold of one end. The carnival had moved on by this time, so it was only Audrey, Oliver and Pete down there. The key was in one of the zip pockets of my jeans, but they only made it half way to the pavement with the clothes-rope at full stretch. Even when Mum added a tablecloth and two tea towels from drawers in the flat it was about four metres short.

'Might help if we had your clothes too!' Dad shouted down.

'We'd get arrested!' Oliver shouted up.

'No you wouldn't! The cops in this town are fakes!'

'Couldn't pass them up anyway unless we had something to tie them to!' Audrey chipped in.

'If you open the door,' Pete said, 'we could just chuck 'em in.'

'Shut up, Pete,' said everyone.

Oliver got Pete to stand on his shoulders and Audrey held Pete's ankles to stop him falling off, but the jeans were still out of reach.

'Well,' Mum said, reaching behind her, 'there's nothing for it.'

'Mum, no!' I cried.

'You've seen them before, Jig,' she said.

'Not without shuddering,' I said.

'Just don't lean out,' Dad told her.

'I wasn't planning to.'

She fixed the bra-thing to the top end of the clothes-rope and Pete, wobbling like a loon on his dad's shoulders, reached up.

'Still...can't...reach!'

There was a pause while Pete fell into Audrey's arms. At the end of the pause, our end, Dad said, 'Jiggy.'

'Hello?'

'You'll have to hold the top end.'

'OK,' I said, taking the clothes-rope from him.

'I'll hold your ankles,' he added.

'You'll what?'

'And lower you out of the window.'

'Lower me out of the window?'

'Don't worry, I won't let go.'

'What if there's a wasp?' Mum said.

'A wasp?' said Dad.

'A wasp might suddenly appear and buzz round your head and you'll wave it away and lose your grip.'

'I won't lose my grip.'

'You might if it attacks you.'

'Bit of a coincidence if a wasp attacked me as I'm holding Jiggy out of the window,' Dad said.

'It's a waspy time of year,' she said.

I had something else on my mind than wasps.

'You want me to hang out of the window in… this?' I said.

'Don't worry,' Dad said. 'The crowd's gone.'

I twitched. My feet started to move. My elbows flapped. This is what happens when I get agitated or nervous. Becomes a problem keeping still. That's why I'm called Jiggy.

'The crowd might have gone,' I said, 'but there's an entire town down there having a carnival. There's a beach. An ocean. Krillions of people in deckchairs and suntan oil who'll immediately look my way with telescopes and zoom lenses. They'll video me for their grandchildren to laugh at years from now, hanging upside down from a window in a Youngman jockstrap.'

'No one asked you to wear it,' Angie said.

'No, they didn't. But when I put it on I didn't know I'd be showing it off to the world and its dog.'

Mum leaned towards me.

'Darling,' she said in that coaxing sort of way that stopped working when I was five.

'Don't darling me,' I said, shuddering and looking away.

She put her hand on my bare shoulder. 'We have to do this, Jig.'

'We?' I shook her off. 'Fine. You do it.'

'Without a bra?' she said.

'Don't remind me, it's not easy finding other places to look.'

Dad grinned happily. 'And I can't do it 'cos I'm too heavy.'

'You wouldn't be if you ate less and took more exercise,' Mum snapped.

'Why can't Angie do it?' I asked.

'Because she's a girl,' Mum said.

I glanced at Angie. You wouldn't think anyone could look so smug in nothing but their vest and pants. All she needed was a plastic halo from Woolworth's.

'You never cared about being a girl before,' I said to her.

'No one ever wanted to hang me upside down out of a window in my undies before,' she said with a sickly-sweet girly smile.

So it was me who climbed on to the ledge. Me, Jiggy McCue, in my glorious little item from the market, which was still flashing all those colours, one after the other.

'Jig, what the hell are you wearing?' Pete yelled up.

'It's his special dangling-from-windows suit!' Angie yelled down.

I was just going over the ledge hoping that whoever invented backless jock straps had also gone out of a window, but without someone gripping his ankles, when the music started. The stall-keeper hadn't told me it was a musical jock that could be set off if you knocked it. It was a wonder it hadn't started when the Big Fat Bunny fell on me, but it hadn't. Did now, though. There I was, my first hour at Wonkton-on-Sea, hanging upside down from the window of our unrented holiday flat, while the chorus of 'YMCA' blasted out of my crotch.

Chapter Five

It wasn't until they hauled me back inside and the others started up with the key, that Angie said, 'Of course, we could have just thrown your jeans down. They wouldn't have gone down the drain.'

Mum and Dad looked at one another with amazement. I looked at them with amazement too. Then they looked at me with amazement. Why hadn't we thought of that? We all looked at Angie with amazement.

'Couldn't you have come up with that before?' I said.

'What, and miss you hanging upside down in mid air in that thing while the Village People entertained us?'

Just before the others let themselves in with the key Mum shut herself in the bathroom. I kept to the kitchen. Angie undid the knots in the clothes-rope and handed Mum's clothes round the bathroom door, then threw mine into the kitchen.

'I don't know what you're hiding for,' she said. 'It's all been seen. By everyone!'

One of the first things Oliver did was take the lock apart. Oliver's a whiz at taking stuff apart. He's not so good at putting it together again, but at least the door didn't stay closed any more. It couldn't, with its lock in ruins on the floor. Audrey pointed out that one of us would have to stay in at all times in case there were burglars. I didn't intend that person to be me. I like my own space, and a holiday flat with six others isn't the place for that, specially when one of them is Pete Garrett, who just would not let the Youngman jockstrap die a peaceful death. I should have slipped out without a word, but I didn't. I announced the fact that I was going out as I made for the door.

'Hey, wait for me,' said Angie.

'And me,' said Pete.

'Where are you going?' Mum asked.

'Just a look around,' I said.

'I'll come with you. I want to see what Wonkton has to offer.'

'So do I,' said Audrey. 'Perhaps we'll find a little café. We haven't eaten since the motorway service station.'

'We could get something at a pub,' Oliver said.

'Good idea,' said Dad. 'Bound to be pubs here if nothing else.'

They all joined me at the door.

'Whoa,' I said. 'What about not leaving the flat unguarded with the door like this?'

'Oh,' said Audrey. 'Yes. One of us had better stay behind.'

But no one volunteered. I sighed.

'I'll stay.'

'Oh, you can't,' said Mum. 'If we're hungry you must be.'

'I'll survive. I saw some biscuits in one of the kitchen cupboards.'

'Well, if you're sure...'

'Yeah. Scoot.'

And off they went, all of them, without me, whose idea it was.

When their feet had stopped clattering happily down the stairs I grabbed a couple of handfuls of biscuits and watched them go down the hill from the main window. I sighed again. All that town, all that sea, and I was indoors, top of a hill, waiting for burglars. I turned the telly on. Two teenage presenters in stupid clothes were jumping up and down and being jolly about nothing. Screaming audience of young kids in the background, whipped up into a frenzy by off-camera nutters holding boards with instructions to CHEER LOUDLY! Bozo TV. I switched channels. A soap. Switched again. Another soap. Switched a third time. Eight people in a room swearing at one another, under bleeps because it was early.

I turned the thing off. Went back to the window.

The more I looked out the more I wanted to be on the other side of the glass, though not as high up. I'd done enough of that for one lifetime. In the end I decided to risk the burglars and go out. I didn't want to encourage them, though. If they saw the door open they'd know they could just trot in and swipe our holiday clothes, but the only way to stop the door from swinging open was to put something behind it, like a chair. Only trouble with that was that if I put a chair behind it I wouldn't be able to get out. But then I had one of my dazzling brainwaves. I found some chewing gum, chewed two sticks in double-quick time, and when it was all soft and tacky I stuck it to the edge of the door.

I went out to the landing and pulled the door after me. The door stayed closed. 'McCue, you're a genius,' I said proudly. Common knowledge, of course, except among my teachers and parents, but I like to hear it.

Outside I started down the hill. By half way I was already not looking forward to coming back up. I mooched into the town. It was an OK sort of town. Not huge, not terrifically interesting, but OK. Sure wasn't JoyWorld. I didn't look round much of it because I didn't want to bump into the others. If Mum saw me she would pull one of her long faces, say: 'I can't trust you to do a thing, can I, Jiggy,' and rush up the hill to stick a chair behind the door.

I headed for the sea.

I like the sea. I like the way it changes all the time. I like beaches too, long as they're not too crowded. This one wasn't crowded, maybe because it wasn't that hot. Warm, sunny, but not sweltering. It was mostly a pebble beach, but there were patches of sand, and it got much sandier near the water. Some kids had built a big castle on one of the sand patches. Nice job. Bucket-shaped towers and all, like I used to make. Pity the tide would come in soon and wash it away.

I took my shoes off and stuck with the patches of sand as much as I could because pebbles under nude feet can hurt. This meant zigzagging around a bit. There were these little rock pools dotted about and I liked dipping my feet in them, even if slimy seaweed got stuck between my toes. I saw a baby crab in one. It didn't get me.

Along the beach a way I saw an ice cream hut. Ooh, I thought, maybe they have Super-Space Fizzers. Super-Space Fizzers are my favourite ice cream. The Super-Space Fizzer looks like a rocket on a stick and it's covered with thick dark chocolate with these tiddly little stars in it, and when you bite or lick through the chocolate there's this multi-coloured ice inside which fizzes on your tongue. It's terrific. I plodded to the hut to clock the board with the sun-bleached pictures of the ice creams and lollies they sold, and saw...a faded Super-Space Fizzer! I felt in my pocket for change.

'Yah?'

This was the woman in the hut. Face like a beefburger, with big red lips and earrings shaped like parrots.

'One Super-Space Fizzer please.'

'Don't got none.'

'Don't got none?'

'It's an old board.'

'Oh.'

'We got others.'

'No. S'all right. Thanks.'

I dropped my money back in my pocket. I walked on. Suddenly all I could think about was Super-Space Fizzers. I'd never wanted a Super-Space Fizzer as much as I wanted one just then.

I was still walking, still tasting the Super-Space Fizzer I didn't have, when I heard these squeaky little voices. I'd been watching my bare feet kicking pebbles, but when I heard the voices I looked up. Just along the beach there was this red-and-white striped tent, taller than a telephone box and twice as wide on all sides, and there were all these little kids sitting in a semi-circle on the other side of it. Hey, I thought, a Punch and Judy show. I hadn't seen a Punch and Judy show since I was so-high. I used to love Punch and Judy. Liked the way they bashed one another with sticks. The way they screamed and kicked each other around. I liked the way the baby got knocked out of its pram. I liked the policeman and the crocodile. Made me hoot, all that. But as I got closer I saw that this one wasn't a Punch and Judy show. A long board on top of the square tent said so.

MR NICEY-NICEY AND MS SWEET

Mr Nicey-Nicey and Ms Sweet? No wonder the kids looked bored. Still, I thought I'd take a decko. I'd taken about five steps before I realised that I couldn't feel sand under my feet any more, or even pebbles. I looked down. I wasn't walking on the beach. I was walking above it. On nothing.

'Uh?'

I was still trying to get used to this when my feet lifted sharply in front of me, swooped up over my head (taking my legs with them) and came down somewhere over my back. I'd done an almost complete somersault without trying and suddenly I was in touch with the beach again. Very in touch. Lying face-down in one of those nice little rock pools, chewing seaweed. I gave Mr Nicey-Nicey and Ms Sweet a miss. Headed back to the flat.

The others got back about an hour after I did.

I was sitting at the window reading a book when they charged in, breathing hard from the climb up the hill and the stairs. Yes, a book. Jiggy McCue was reading a book. I was desperate, all right? Nothing else to do.

'What's it like?' I said as they came in.

'What's what like?' said Angie.

'Wonkton-on-Sea.'

'It's like a seaside town with nothing in it, that's what it's like.'

'There are quite a lot of shops,' her mother said.

'Shops!' said Angie.

'And the beach looks nice.'

'Beach!'

I didn't say I'd been to the beach. I couldn't. I was supposed to have been minding the flat. Because I couldn't say I'd been to the beach I couldn't tell Pete and Angie about the somersault into the rock pool, even though I wanted to. I didn't understand that somersault. I'd never done a somersault in my life before. That's why I'd been reading the book. To try and put it out of my mind. Out of your mind is always the best place for things you don't understand, I always say.

'What are we going to do all week?' Pete said, throwing himself onto the floor.

'You could try and perfect that floor dive,' I said.

Oliver wasn't too happy when he found that Mum and Dad had already bagged the biggest and best bedroom. 'Cut you for it,' he said to Dad. So they cut the cards they'd brought with them for boring evenings at JoyWorld. Dad won. Nothing changed.

There were twin beds in the second bedroom, so Angie shared with her mum and Oliver was stuck with the couch in the living room, which opened out into a bed. He didn't seem too sad about that, probably because the living room was where the TV was, and the TV had a couple of sports channels he could watch all night if he couldn't sleep ('So long as you keep the sound *right* down,' Audrey told him).

My room was the worst. It was the worst because it was the smallest and pokiest and because it had bunk-beds, and I would have to share with Pete. I made the mistake of not planting my flag on the top bunk right off, because when Garrett saw which room he was in he climbed up on it and said:

'This is mine!'

'I saw it first,' I said.

'I *sat* on it first.'

I bared my teeth at him. 'Fight you for it.'

He threw a pillow at me. I ducked and the pillow knocked over this stupid little table thing, which brought Mum running in.

'Jiggy, be careful, this isn't our property.'

By the time I got halfway through explaining, I'd lost interest in who had which bunk, so Pete kept the top one.

By evening we were pretty whacked. All of us, even the Golden Oldies. It had been a long and mostly disappointing day. So we turned in early. I don't know what time it was when I had the dream, but it went like this. I heard a sound. I opened my eyes. I was in this long box sort of thing with the sides missing, in a dark room I didn't recognise, and there, across the room, stood this little doll.

'Are you awake?' the doll said. Its voice was high-pitched and small, but male.

'Wha?' I said.

There's not a lot else you can say when you've just dreamed you've been woken up by a doll in a big box in a strange room. I couldn't make him out too well because of the dark. Not that I needed to. The dream would be over in a mo and I'd move on to the next one and forget this one. I sat up. In the dream. Overhead, on top of my box, I heard heavy breathing. Probably some monster waiting to gobble me up if the dream didn't finish soon.

'What do you want?' I asked the doll.

'I need your help,' he said.

'My help? Why?'

'Because of what you did to me.'

'I've never done anything to you. I've never seen you before. Can't see you now too well.'

'If you can't see me now, how do you know you haven't seen me before?'

'Call it a wild guess.'

He drew himself up to his full height, which wasn't much.

'It's your fault I'm like this,' he said.

'My fault?'

'Oh, don't come the innocent.'

'I haven't the faintest idea what you're talking about. All I know is you're spoiling my dream. Push off.'

'Dream?' the doll said. 'You think this is a dream? It's no dream. It's a friddling nightmare, that's what it is.'

'Yeah, well I don't want a nightmare. Vanish. Skedaddle. Go back where you came from and leave me in — '

'Peace' was the word I would have said if something big and lumpy hadn't swung down from the top of my dream box and smacked me in the snout.

'Give it a rest, McCue, I'm trying to sleep up here.'

I looked into the shadows where the dream doll had been. It wasn't there any more.

Chapter Six

Next morning, Sunday morning, Mum said we needed milk. She and Audrey had picked up a few things while they were out yesterday, but they hadn't bought enough milk for everyone's cereals and tea and coffee and...milk. Which meant that I was expected to go and get some, like somebody who has nothing better to do with his time.

'You think I've got nothing better to do with my time than go and get milk?' I said when she told me.

'I don't know,' she said. 'Have you got something better to do with your time?'

'I might have.'

'Go and get the milk, Jiggy.'

'We've got enough if we go easy.'

'We don't want to go easy. We're on holiday from going easy. Another litre and we'll have ample.'

'I don't want to go out,' I said.

She turned her lips into a spout. 'Everything's

too much trouble for you, isn't it?'

'Not everything. I eat chocolate pudding without complaining.'

'Jiggy, it's just down the road.'

'Mother, it's down the hill. A very steep hill. A steep hill which has to be come back up afterwards. With heavy milk.'

'Why do you always have to argue with me?' she said. 'I do a lot of things for you without arguing.'

'It's your role in life,' I reminded her. 'You're a mother.'

'I'll go,' Angie piped up.

I turned to her. 'Keep out of this.'

'It's no big deal,' she said. 'It's only milk.'

'I know it's only milk. I was just going to go and get it.'

'Well why didn't you say so in the first place instead of arguing?'

'It's a boy thing,' I said, snatching the money from my mother.

I started downstairs. Parents. Always wanting stuff. Self, self, self. And you can't do a thing about it. I won't be visiting them very often in the home I put them in when they're fifty. And I won't take grapes. Or stay long. That'll teach 'em.

Halfway down the stairs I saw that the door to Flat 1 was open. Not open much, but enough to see in without bending your neck out of shape. It looked pretty much like our flat. Nothing special, nothing fancy, just a flat. There was a Golden Oldie in there, bending over a table doing some paperwork or something. Fascinating. I carried on down.

It was warmer out today, even though it was only morning still. Looked like being a real hotty. Good day to stay indoors if there'd been anything to do there. I noticed a small van by the kerb outside Journey's End. I couldn't have missed it if I tried. The sun bounced off its red-and-white stripes like it wanted to blind me. There was a sign on top of the van. *Shanks Shows*. I started down the hill.

Fortunately I didn't have to go all the way to the bottom. Halfway down there was the little foody shop Mum had told me about. I threw back the door.

'Good morning,' a voice sang out.

'That was last week,' I sang back.

I found my way to a tall fridge with a glass door and let my eyes jog along the milk labels. Then I checked the list in my hand. The list only had one thing on it — 'milk, semi-skimmed' — but I needed to be absolutely sure because there was no semi-skimmed in the fridge.

'Any semi-skimmed?' I asked the girl at the counter.

'No, sorry. There was a run on it yesterday and the fresh milk hasn't been delivered yet.'

Problem. My mother has to have semi-skimmed milk. Any other kind just won't do. And because she has to have it so does everyone else, including me. Even Stallone has to have it. I don't think Stallone likes semi-skimmed. Usually leaves half a saucer and slinks off with his tail thumping. Thing was, they didn't have semi-skimmed at this shop. What was I supposed to do? Trundle back up half a hill and ask my mother if she would settle, just this once, for some other kind? If I did that she might say no and send me further down the hill, to another shop, which would mean at least twice the climb up, plus the half I'd already done to ask what I should do. I grabbed a plastic bottle of 'whole milk'. If she didn't like it she could water it down.

By the time I made it back to the top of the hill I was wheezing like I was on my way to my ninety-first birthday party. I'm about as good at climbing hills as I am at running. The running skill shortage annoys my PE teacher, Mr Rice. Old Ricipops seems to think that a leg isn't a leg unless it's moving quickly. Specially if it's a boy's leg. Specially on the football pitch. I'm not a terrific football fan. Yeah, yeah, I know, I'm a boy, I shouldn't admit stuff like that. It's like the Pope saying he prefers cream cakes to religion. My dad can't understand it. Nor can Mr Rice. When we're on the footie pitch at school and I stop running and stand with my hands on my knees gasping for breath, Rice thinks I'm pulling a fast one. Fast? Me? On the football pitch? 'You have long legs, McCue!' he yells. 'Use 'em! Pick 'em up, pick 'em up!' Cretin.

The stripy van was still outside Journey's End. The rear doors were open now. There was someone in there, moving about, but I didn't stop to see who it was because (a) it took all my concentration to drag air into my lungs, and (b) I wasn't interested.

I went through the archway to the little courtyard and after a bit of a breath break started up the stairs. Up, up, up. Was there no end to this? What did the world think I was, a mountaineer? Halfway up, on the little platform outside the door of Flat 1, I stopped for another breather. The door was even more open now, so naturally I glanced in again. No sign of the bloke who lived there this time. Probably him in the van down in the street, I thought. I was about to continue my climb when I heard voices. Very small voices.

'Hello?' I said.

The voices stopped. Then there was this scampering sound, like mice racing for cover when a cat appears. Then that stopped too.

I leaned into the flat. Swung my head around. No one there. I glanced down the stairs. The man might start up any second, but I decided to take a chance. It's not every day you hear voices in an empty room. I went in. Not far, just a step. I only wanted a quick look. Didn't plan on flopping into an armchair and putting my feet up. One step in I stopped, listening hard. There wasn't a sound. Not a peep. Until...

'It's you,' a squeaky little voice said.

I swung my head again. Still no one. I stepped further in. The room was definitely empty. But then...the door started to close.

'Woh!'

I turned to run. I could get into trouble if whoever was behind the door caught me. But I didn't run because I could already see who it was. What it was.

The doll from last night's dream!

I hadn't seen his face then because it was dark, but I knew it was him. Had to be. And there was something else. I'd seen that little red bowler hat and yellow waistcoat before. Somewhere.

'Placed me yet?' the doll said.

'Placed you?' I was in a bit of a daze, if you want to know.

'Who I am.'

'I...I thought I dreamt you.'

'Well you didn't. I'm real. You want it in writing?'

I took a quick look outside to make sure the man wasn't coming up yet, then dropped to one knee.

'You're amazing,' I said.

The doll frowned. 'Amazing how?'

'I mean since when could dolls talk back?'

The frown became a scowl. 'Watch who you're calling a doll.'

'Talk back, change their expressions, move their arms...'

'And their feet,' he said.

'Their feet?'

He ran at me and kicked me in the kneecap I wasn't kneeling on. Hard. I yelled and sat back on my rear end.

'Next time you call me a doll it's your head,' he said.

It was when he said that, and while I was nursing the pain in my knee, that I got it. Got him.

'You're the character from the market stall back home. The one who sold my mother the underpants that made my life a misery.'*

'The very same,' he said. 'Took a while, kid, but you got there in the end.'

'But you can't be him. I mean he was...'

'Normal-size?'

'Almost.'

'I wasn't normal-size the last time you saw me.'

---

* For the full tragic story read *The Killer Underpants*.

78

'No. That's right. I forgot.'

'You forgot. You do this to me, make me the size of a bonsai tree, and just turn around and get on with your life like I never happened? How nice for you.'

'You're really him?' I said. 'You're not a doll?'

'I'm really him.'

'Are you still…evil?'

'I do my best,' he said. 'Well, my worst. But you can't be truly evil when dogs pick you up and carry you off in their jaws.'

'Has that happened?'

'Once. It won't happen again. Not with that dog.'

'Why not?'

'I turned it into a beetle and jumped on it.'

'So you still have some magic.'

'That's not magic. I'm not a magician. I'm a devil. Devils can do stuff. Trouble is, when you're this small the only stuff you can do isn't so huge. I miss the huge stuff.'

A sound from downstairs. The main door opening. The man who lived here was coming up. I got off the floor in a hurry.

'Gotta go.'

'No, wait,' he said. 'I need your help. That's why you're here.'

'Why I'm here?' I said from the doorway.

'Yes. You don't think I set all this up for my friddling health, do you?'

There was a twist in the stairs below. Footsteps on the twist.

'Some other time. Bye.'

I shot up the stairs, forgetting they were steep and exercise is bad for you. In the flat I handed the non-semi-skimmed to my mother and sat down with my hands over my ears while she gave them the hammering I knew she would. I didn't bother telling her it was the only milk in the shop. I had other things on my mind now.

Chapter Seven

My mother isn't so great. Oh, she thinks she is, but she's not so hot. Just because she organises everything. Just because she dusts the house and fluffs up the cushions. Just because she does the ironing and cleans the floors and the lousy brass. Just because she buys our clothes and washes them. Just because she buys things like soap and dishwasher tablets. Just because she gets the food in and cooks it and puts out Stallone's Rats Thighs in Vegetarian Gravy. Just because she makes sure the bills are paid. Just because she mows the lawn and sorts the garden and arranges the holidays. She isn't so perfect. She makes mistakes. Like forgetting to pack two of our three toothbrushes. Not hers. Oh, no, she's all right. Her toothbrush is neatly stowed in her dinky little washbag with her flannel and nail-polish remover. But what about Dad's and mine? (Our toothbrushes, not our nail-polish remover.) Ours don't count. Our toothbrushes are still at home, in the bathroom, side by side, not talking.

'You forgot our toothbrushes?' I said when she realised she hadn't packed them. 'Last night you said you couldn't find them, but today you remember you forgot them. Why didn't you remember last night?'

'Last night I thought I might have put them in with something else, but I've completely unpacked now and I obviously didn't. Sorry.'

'Sorry? Sorry doesn't clean my teeth. Sorry doesn't put toothpaste on a non-existent brush. Sorry just does not hack it, Mother.'

The brush shortage meant I had to make do with toothpaste on a finger.* The taste was the same, but for the first time in my life I missed that brush. My mother said she'd pick one up later.

'Two,' said Dad. 'Remember me?'

'Just makes sure they're new ones,' I told her. 'Stay away from charity shops.'

'What shall we do today then?' Audrey asked after breakfast. She wasn't talking about toothbrushes. No need to. She had hers too.

 * One of mine; Mum refused.

'There just better not be a model village here,' Pete whispered.

'Or clock golf,' said Ange.

'And we definitely don't want a seven-person picnic,' I said.

I hadn't told them what happened earlier. I was trying to stuff it into the back of my mind with all the other junk I don't want to think about, like unplanned somersaults. I tell you, if some mind explorer ever gets in there and finds a way through the cobwebs with a torch he'll find all sorts of rubbish I've stowed there over the years.

'I'd like to get some of that sun on my skin,' Mum said.

'Me too,' said Audrey.

'I'd like to stick to the shade,' said Dad.

'Me too,' said Ollie.

'What about you kids?' Mum asked.

'Are we allowed to go off on our own?' I said.

She looked at Audrey. Audrey looked at her. They thought about this together without actually saying anything.

'If they stick to the town?' Audrey said to her.

'And watch the roads,' said Mum.

'And stay together,' said Audrey.

'If you stick to the town, watch the roads and stay together,' Mum said to us.

'What if we want to come back here?' Angie asked.

'Why would we want to do that?' said Pete. He thought the flat was the pits. It wasn't that bad, but it wasn't the sort of place you'd want to spend your entire holiday in.

'We might want to get out of the sun,' Angie said.

'Did you put the lock back together?' Audrey asked Oliver.

'Yeah. Good as new.'

'Does that mean we can open the door from the inside now?'

'You think I didn't test that before shutting the door?'

'How would I know? Men's minds are a mystery to me.'

Ollie smirked. 'That's why we're the rulers of the planet.'

Audrey scowled. 'That's why we have all these wars.'

'I meant,' Angie said, 'how do we get back in without a key?'

The mothers thought about this. 'We'll have to hide it.'

'Hide it?' said Pete. 'We don't want to have to search for it.'

'Hide it somewhere we all know about but burglars won't,' said Mum.

So we all trooped downstairs and looked for somewhere to hide the key. There wasn't much choice. It was only a concrete yard for a couple of cars. The only hiding places were a few big pot plants.

'Have to be under one of those then,' Audrey said.

'First place burglars look, plant pots,' said Dad.

'There probably won't be any burglars anyway,' said Mum.

'If there won't be any burglars why are we hiding the key?'

'I didn't say there won't be any burglars, only that there probably won't be. Security precaution, that's all.'

'Not a great one,' said Dad.

After we left them we stood in the street outside Journey's End wondering what to do next until I suggested we look round the town.

'Done that,' said Pete.

'I haven't.' It wasn't really a lie. I hadn't seen much of the town.

'Well two out of three of us have, so you're outnumbered.'

'We could look again,' said Angie.

'What at?' Pete said. 'There's nothing to see.'

'Go back to the flat then,' I said.

'And spend even more time with the Golden Oldies? I'd rather walk round this manky town again.'

'So what are you arguing for?'

'Who's arguing?'

So we mooched round Wonkton, round and round and up and down, trying to forget the place where we should be right now instead of here. There were quite a few shops. Most of them weren't up to much, like the one called Bygone Days that sold all this manky old rubbish, and Glitterati, which sold all this manky new rubbish, but at least they were different from the ones back home. There was a bread shop with cakes and pies in the windows, and Pete and I went in for a bag of dinky doughnuts each. They also sold these potato cake things which the ticket said were Irish Farls. I liked that. Irish Farls. Sounded like rioting tribesmen in kilts. We passed an amusement arcade, and a place that did milk-shakes with curly straws, and a little cinema, very old-fashioned-looking, with nothing on that we wanted to see all week. Angie wanted to go in a record shop but Pete said she wasn't allowed. She asked why not. He pointed to the sign on the door. *Guide Dogs Only*. She hit him.

There were about six pubs, so Dad and Ollie would have somewhere to go if they ever left the flat. One of the pubs was called The Hog's Head, except two of the aitches and the apostrophe had scarpered, so it looked like The Ogs Ead. A brass plate beside the door of some offices got a laugh. CRIMINAL SOLICITORS. 'Wouldn't think they'd want people to know, would you?' Angie said. There was also a wax museum called Wax Works, but you couldn't see in to this without paying money at the desk the other side of the glass doors and actually going in.

Next door to Wax Works was the one window in town that chopped Pete's onions. It didn't do much for Ange and me, but the moment Pete saw it (he'd missed it somehow on his previous tour) he slammed his nose against the glass. Striker's Magic Joke Shop, it was called. 'Look at that!' He fingered the window to show us the thing that most took his fancy. The Combo Fun Box. There were other jokey things there, like famous-people masks and vampire outfits, stuff like that, but it was The Combo Fun Box that did it for Pete. 'That I've got to have,' he said, going through his pockets. When he looked at the money he found there he turned to us. 'We could club together.'

'We're too old for that sort of stuff,' Angie said.

'You might be,' he said.

'Look in the corner, Pete. What does it say?'

'Glow-in-the-dark Super Realistic Snot.'

'Next to that. The age it's intended for.'

'What, 6-plus?'

'6-plus. If you haven't noticed, you're not six any more.'

'No, but I'm plus,' he said. 'The plus could be up to a hundred and four. Come on, buy it with me.'

'No.'

'Jig?' I shook my head. 'But look what it's got in it!' He scanned the list on the lid of The Combo Fun Box. 'Itching powder, fake blood, super-hot sweets, an ice cube with a fly in it, a shock pen, three fake moustaches, black soap, exploding gum – '

Angie and I walked away. We'd got about fifty metres before Pete realised he was reading aloud to a wad of pensioners who'd just zimmered off a coach.

'The fake tattoos'd be a hoot,' he said when he caught us up. 'We could let the Oldies think we'd had our entire arms done. Imagine their faces!'

'Let's go to the beach,' I said.

'What for?' Angie said.

'I like beaches.'

'Is nobody listening to me?' said Pete.

'Let's go to the beach,' said Ange.

We went to the beach.

Chapter Eight

The beach wasn't crowded yet, obviously because it was quite early still. Most people would be waiting till the sun got really hot so they could run out and throw themselves on a patch of sand, or some pebbles, and ruin their skin in the shortest possible time. We stopped talking when we passed two lady sunbathers on towels. You couldn't miss them. They were lying face down with their heads under a sunshade, and they had these thong things on. Just that, thong things between two pairs of doughnuts. Not dinky ones either.

'Cheeky,' I whispered.

'Double cheeky,' Pete whispered back.

'Reminds me of you yesterday,' Angie whispered to me.

I waited till we were far enough away from the Thong Creatures of Wonkton before asking Angie to do me a favour.

'What's that, Jig?'

'Never ever − I mean *ever* − mention yesterday again.'

'OK,' she said. 'Youngman.'

I made a swipe at her. She ducked.

Then we just strolled, the three of us, kicking sand and pebbles. It was good, strolling along the beach. Strolling along beaches isn't something we do a lot of back home on the Brook Farm Estate. We did this until Pete saw the ice cream hut that didn't sell Super-Space Fizzers and swerved towards it. The burger-faced lady with the big lips and parrot earrings was just going in the side door to open up for the day. As we sauntered after Pete, I heard Angie singing, very quietly, the chorus I never wanted to hear again in my life.

'Angie Mint!' I said sternly.

'Sorry,' she said. 'You know how it is when you get a song in your head. Just won't go away. And...funny thing.'

'What?'

'I can't seem to separate the song from the image of your bum hanging out the window.'

Pete had just finished scanning the faded ice creams and lollies on the board when we caught up with him.

'They've got Mister Kreemies!' he said.

I told him not to count on it. He asked the woman how soon she'd be open.

'Soon as I'm ready,' she answered.

'Which is, like, when?'

'Soon as I'm ready,' she snapped.

'Come back in a minute,' Angie said to Pete.

From there I steered them to the bit of sand I'd done the somersault on, with the little rock pool I'd landed face down in. I wanted to see if the same thing happened to them. When we got there I stopped suddenly and looked around like I was admiring the view.

'Why have we stopped?' Pete asked.

'I'm admiring the view.'

'What view?'

'The sea. The beach.'

'It's just sea. Just a beach. And it smells bad.'

'Seaweed,' said Angie.

'Seaweed yourself,' said Pete.

I stayed put, so they stayed put with me. But nothing happened. No somersaults. Not even a little skip. Not a hiccup.

We walked on. Just ahead was the not-quite

Punch and Judy booth I'd seen yesterday. The man who ran it was getting things ready for the first show of the day. He must have just put the booth up because if it had been there all night it would have been a heap of red-and-white-striped ashes by now. Everything gets vandalised if it's left unguarded for long enough. The man must have heard us because he looked up.

'Hey,' he said. 'You kids want to do me a favour?' We headed towards him. 'I forgot a couple of things. Have to go back home for them and I need someone to watch my gear.'

'How much?' said Pete.

'How much?'

'To watch your gear.'

'Oh. Well. Um.'

Angie kicked Pete sideways. 'He's joking. Real joker, old Pete.'

The man laughed. 'How about seeing the show for free?' he said to Joker Pete. 'That cover it?'

Pete rubbed his ankle. 'What do you think we are — seven?'

Angie pushed him behind her out of harm's way. 'That'd be great.'

But even though he'd asked us, and even though one of us had said we'd do it, suddenly the man didn't seem too sure.

'Just for ten minutes,' he said.

'Take your time,' said Ange.

'You're sure it's OK?'

'Absolutely.'

'I mean one or two of the puppets in here are quite...unique. Hate to lose them.'

'We'll watch out for them,' Angie said.

Still he didn't go. Obvious why. We were kids. He'd only asked us to watch his stuff because we happened to be around, but then he'd thought, 'They could swipe my puppets. They could torch my booth. They could ruin me.' If we were adults he wouldn't have worried. If we were Martians he probably wouldn't have worried. Kids, though – risky!

But Angie must have got it across that she could be trusted even if her friends couldn't. Angie can make anyone trust her when she wants. The man nodded, gave a weak smile, and headed for the road that ran along the top of the beach. We watched him go. Watched him climb the steps to a van parked on the road.

'I know that van,' I said. 'It was outside Journey's End when I went for the milk.'

'Outside where?' said Pete.

'Place we're staying.'

'What makes you think it was that van?' Angie asked.

'Well, I could be wrong. There could be a million red-and-white-striped vans round here with *Shanks Shows* on top.'

'Same stripes as this,' she said, meaning the Mr Nicey-Nicey and Ms Sweet booth.

'Yes,' I said. Then I said, 'Uh?'

I said, 'Uh?' because my feet had just whipped out in front of me, wooshed up into the air, and flipped me over. When I came down my face went straight into a rock pool. Different rock pool from yesterday, but still a rock pool.

'Thirsty?' said Pete, glancing back as I lifted my head.

'Did you…' I spat salt water. 'Did you see that?'

'See what?'

'I flipped. Right over.'

'You flipped at birth,' he said, turning back to the booth.

I struggled to my feet, spluttering. Looked around for some clue to why somersaults would occur. There was nothing. My feet started to move. My elbows went up. My arms started flapping like a poltergoose's wings.

Angie noticed.

'What now?' she said.

'Bad feeling,' I said, dancing and flapping, flapping and dancing.

She curled her lip. 'You and your bad feelings.'

'Don't knock it. I had a bad feeling before we missed the plane, didn't I?'

'Coincidence.'

I forced my feet to stand still. Pulled the McCue elbows into the McCue ribs.

'Well don't just stand there,' said a small voice from nowhere.

Pete and Angie's eyebrows lifted. I think mine did too, but not in surprise like theirs. A bit of truth had just dawned. I went round to the front of the booth.

There was a notice. This notice.

PROFESSOR SHANKS
Presents
THE FAMOUS
PUNCH & JUDY
SHOW

'Where are you?' I said.

'In here, where d'you think?'

Quite high up in the top half of the booth these little red curtains were pulled across the stage where the action took place. I lifted one of the curtains to look under it. Something came out of the dark and slugged me across the nose. I yelped and flew backwards.

'What's happening?' Angie said, sprinting round the corner followed by Pete.

Instead of answering I marched to back to the booth and yanked the curtains back. And there he was, the itsy character from downstairs in his little red bowler and yellow waistcoat – holding the miniature rolling pin that had just bopped my conk.

'That got your attention, didn't it,' he said, resting the rolling pin on his shoulder.

'What's this?' Angie said, staring at him.

'Looks like the little slimeball from the market that time,' said Pete.

'I am the little slimeball from the market that time,' the tiny man said.

'But you're so...small,' Angie said.

'Now I wonder whose fault *that* is?' he snapped back.

'You mean you're actually him?' said Pete.

The itsy man bowed. 'Neville the Devil at your service – again.'

'*That's* the name!' I said, smacking my forehead.

'Aren't you cute,' Angie said, prodding his dinky little waistcoat.

'Cute?' Neville said.

'Sweet,' said Angie.

'Sweet?' said Neville.

'Very,' said Angie.

Whump!

This was the little rolling pin coming down on Angie's head.

Chapter Nine

The miniature Neville the Devil glared at us from the little stage. 'Now lend me your ears,' he said. 'I have work for you three.'

'Work?' I said. 'We're on holiday.'

'No, you're not. You're here to do my bidding.'

'Think again, freak,' said Pete. 'The only bidding we do is teachers', and we don't do that if we can wangle our way out of it.'

Neville raised the rolling pin. 'You want some of this too?'

'No one's getting any more of this,' Angie said, snatching the pin out of his hands.

'Not so cute and sweet now, is he?' I said to her.

'I'll have a lump,' she said, touching the top of her head tenderly.

'I'll probably get a scar,' I said, feeling my nose.

'You kids are pathetic,' said Neville.

'You're the one working in a Punch and Judy show,' Pete said.

'Who says I'm working here?'

'If you're not, what are you, the janitor?'

Neville scowled at him. 'I don't think I like you.'

'I *know* I don't like you,' said Pete.

'If you're not working here what are you doing here?' I asked Neville.

'All right, OK, I'm working here, satisfied? But for my food and somewhere to stay, not for my health or the fun of it.'

'What does your food come in?' Pete said. 'Baby jars?'

'Gimme back that rolling pin!' Neville yelled.

Angie didn't give it back. 'What's this bidding you said we have to do?' she asked.

'Did I say bidding?' He laughed. It was a bad laugh. 'I mean I need your help.'

'Help is better,' she said.

He'd mentioned the help thing before, but only to me, and as the others didn't know this wasn't the first time I'd met him in Wonkton I made like it was news to me too.

'I'm not helping him,' I said. 'After what he put me through that other time? No chance.'

'It's because of that other time that I need the

help,' Neville said. 'That was when you three made me the size I am now. The size I have to stay until those responsible put me right. Which means you.'

'What do we get out of it?' Pete said. It's always a deal with Pete.

Neville raised a tiny eyebrow. 'How about my undying gratitude?'

'Don't need it.'

'My personal friendship?'

'Ditto.'

'I could stop you from turning into a snail.'

'How would you do that?'

'By not making it happen.'

Pete laughed. 'Little squirt like you. You couldn't.'

'Careful, Pete,' I said.

'No, it's a free country,' said Neville. 'Let him speak his mind.'

He leant forward. He was about level with the top of our heads, which is how he'd managed to give Angie's such a crack.

'Say it again, kid.'

'I said a little squirt like you couldn't turn me into a snail,' said Pete.

'Now why would I want to turn you into a snail?' Neville said.

'You said it, not me.'

'That was before I had the better idea.'

'What better idea?'

Neville lifted his tiny bowler hat. There were two warty little stumps underneath. We'd seen those stumps before. We'd seen them develop points too, like they did now, and grow into horns, like they also did now. Angie and I gulped. Pete didn't gulp. Last time he'd turned and run when he saw them. This time Neville was so small he wasn't going to let himself be scared.

Neville raised the hand that wasn't holding the hat. He tweaked one of his horns between the thumb and a finger and winked with the opposite eye. Then he put his hat straight and grinned at us.

'Well?' said Pete.

'Well what?' said Neville.

'Is that it?'

'That's it.'

Pete looked down at himself. Laughed. 'I see no difference.'

'It might take a minute,' Nev said.

102

Pete waited for fifteen seconds.

'Nothing happening – weed.'

'You don't think?' said Neville.

'What I think,' said Pete, 'it that you're a fake. A very small fake. I think you're about as much of a devil as my left thu...'

He was going to say 'about as much of a devil as my left thumb,' and had jerked his thumb up to prove it. He didn't finish 'thumb' because something about it caught his eye. What caught his eye was that his thumb was no longer what it had been all its life. It was a carrot.

Pete's jaw smacked his chest as the fingers of the same hand also turned into carrots. He looked at his other hand. Five more, growing as we watched. He turned to us, close to panic. As he did so his nose also became a carrot.

'There might be more...' said Neville.

Something inside Pete's shorts gave a little jump.

'No!'

He tugged at the bands of his jeans and underpants. Looked inside.

'Nooooo!'

Ange and I leaned forward. Pete let go of the

bands. *Snap, snap.* I didn't blame him. A boy's carrot is private.

'Why carrots?' I asked Neville.

'Vegetables are good for you,' he said. 'So's fruit.'

'Fruit?'

'Jig,' said Angie, nudging me.

I looked where she was looking. Pete looked too. The toes sticking out of his holiday sandals were evolving. Into strawberries.

'Veg and fruit,' I said. I was quite impressed actually.

'It's sort of ongoing,' said Neville.

'Ongoing?'

'Yeah. Once a dinkoon is cast – '

'A what?'

'A dinkoon. Small devilish spell. Once a dinkoon is cast it spreads like a virus until it's run its course.'

While we were talking Pete just stood there with his carrots out (well, the ones on his hands and face), watching his strawberry toes ripen. After the toes his kneecaps became a pair of pears.

'Run its course, you say?' Angie said. 'How long is a course?'

'Depends how nice the victim is to me,' said Neville.

'I'm expected to be nice to you after this?' said Pete.

'Up to you, kiddo.'

Pete's ears grew larger, folded in upon themselves, and turned into...

'Cauliflower ears!' I said.

Pete couldn't see the caulis, but he could feel them.

'Stop!' he wailed. 'Stop! Stop!'

'You know what to do,' said Neville.

'Never!' said Pete.

His shirt filled out at the chest. The buttons pulled apart – *bling, bling, bling!* – and where his scrawny chest had been, there was...

'A cabbage!' I said.

'A Savoy!' said Angie. Know-all.

'All right!' said Pete. 'I'll be nice to you! Worm!'

'That doesn't sound so nice,' said Neville as the carrot that used to be Pete's nose turned mouldy before his eyes. *Right* before his eyes.

Pete was almost sobbing now.

'What do I have to do? Tell me what I have to do.'

'You could try grovelling,' Neville said.

Pete fell to his knees. 'I'm grovelling, I'm grovelling!'

'And asking for my forgiveness.'

'Forgive me! I'll never be rotten to you again!'

'Talking of rotten...' I said.

His strawberry toes had gone all mushy. His carroty fingers were looking kind of old too. Noticing the wrinkly old carrots Pete jumped up in horror. He looked inside his pants.

'NO!'

'Past its sell-by?' I said.

'It's wearing off, isn't it?' Angie said.

'It's gonna *fall* off!' said Pete.

'I mean the spell. The...what did you call it?'

'The dinkoon,' said Neville.

'I reckon you don't have to be nice to him,' Angie said. 'I reckon these dinkoons only last a few minutes, then everything returns to normal. Am I right?' she said to Neville.

'How would I know?' he said. 'I'm just a little cutey. A little sweetie.'

'I withdraw all that,' Angie said. 'You're not cute and you're not sweet. You're just small. And obnoxious.'

'Careful, Ange,' I said.

Angie snapped the little rolling pin in half and tossed it over her shoulder. She glared at Neville.

'He'd better not pick on *me* again.'

Neville looked a bit worried for a second. But just one second.

'If you're all nice to me from now on I'll keep the dinkoons under my bowler. You have my word.'

'And how much is *that* worth?' I asked.

'When a devil gives his word he keeps it,' he said. 'He has no choice if he wants to stay in the Society of Devils. Rule 156a in *The Devil's Handbook*, if you want to look it up.'

In less than a minute Pete was back to normal. Normal for Pete, that is.

'I suppose it was you who made me do the somersaults,' I said to Neville.

He grinned nastily. 'I thought it might make you sit up.'

'Sit up? I was flat on my face in salt water, with crabs.'

'Is that what you did back there?' Angie said. 'A somersault?'

'It's what he *made* me do.'

'You said somersaults. You only did one.'

'No, there was a…' I shook my head. I wasn't in the mood for explanations. I turned back to Neville. 'Why are the words on the front of this booth thing different from the words on top?'

'The Prof forgot the Velcro cover for the front,' Neville said. 'That's one of the things he went back for.'

'The Velcro cover has "Mr Nicey-Nicey and Ms Sweet" on it?'

'Right. It's a requirement if he wants to keep his licence.'

'So it's not really a Punch and Judy show,' Angie said.

'It's a Neville and Judy show, but I don't get a name-check. Judy's another thing he forgot. He's getting absent-minded in his old age. Personally, I wish he'd get even more absent-minded and forget her every time.'

'What happened to Mr Punch?' I asked.

'He's away on an anger management course,' Neville said.

'You talk about him like he's real,' said Angie.

'Of course he's real. What do you think he is, a puppet?'

'Well – yes.'

'Shows what you know. Our Mr P is one angry dude.'

'That's what kids like about him,' I said. 'He's always losing it. That's what makes him so funny.'

'There's no place in the modern world for the likes of Mr Punch,' Neville said. 'It's all got to be cuddly-wuddly now.'

'So who's Mr Nicey-Nicey?'

'Who'd you think?' he snarled.

'You?' I laughed. Couldn't help it. 'You're Mr Nicey-Nicey?'

'Keep laughing, kid, and I'll turn you into something.'

I canned the laughter. 'No offence. It's just the idea of you pretending to be a nice puppet.'

He calmed down. 'You're right. It's not me. That's the problem. That's why I need y – '

'He's coming back!' Angie said.

We looked up the beach. The striped van had returned.

'You had to keep gassing, didn't you?' Nev said. 'All the stuff I need to tell you, but yammer-yammer-yammer, and now it's got to wait, and I'm stuck here for a whole other day. Thanks a heap!'

'But he knows you're human, doesn't he?' Angie said. 'Your master, or whatever he is?'

'Master?' said Neville, rearing up in fury. 'I have no master! And human? Me? How dare you! I'm not one of you! I am...' − he stuck his weenie little chest out − 'a devil!'

'I just meant that he, whatever you call him, knows you're alive,' Angie said.

Neville simmered down. 'He knows. But I'm not supposed to let on to anyone else. You never spoke to me, right? You have no idea I'm not a puppet.' He drew the curtains on himself just in time.

'Everything all right?' said the man Neville had called the Prof.

'Fine,' said Angie.

He looked around to make sure and straight away saw something we'd forgotten about. He put down the big bag he was carrying and picked up the two halves of the tiny rolling pin.

'This is one of my props. Was one of my props.' He eyed us suspiciously. 'You know anything about it?'

'We were just standing here,' Angie said, all

innocent, 'and it came out of the booth like someone had thrown it. Just fell, I suppose.'

'Just fell...' He glanced at the closed curtains. Pretty obvious what he was thinking.

'We'd better be going,' Angie said.

'Before you do,' our new friend said, 'I ought to introduce myself.' He bowed low and flung one arm out, twiddling it at the wrist. 'Armitage Shanks, Professor of Puppetry.'

'Angie, Pete and Jiggy,' said Ange. 'Take your pick who's who.'

'Charmed. The offer stands about coming to the show, you know. Whenever you like. Performances at eleven, one-thirty and three every afternoon, including today.'

'Might take you up on that,' Angie said as we skedaddled.

'Might?' I said when we were far enough away. 'We have *got* to see Neville in action as Mr Nicey-Nicey.'

'I haven't,' said Pete.

We might have gone another way from there, but Pete noticed that the ice cream hut was open and lumbered towards it, instantly forgetting that

111

a couple of minutes ago he'd been Fruit 'n' Veg Boy.

Ange and I followed, in less of a hurry. I only wanted a Super-Space Fizzer and they didn't have any.

There were others queuing for ices too now. The lady sunbathers in thongs. They had their backs to us and the awning of the hut covered their heads, which meant we could look as much as we wanted at their oiled doughnuts gleaming in the sun. Not that Angie wanted.

'You wouldn't catch me in one of those,' she said.

'I wouldn't want to,' I said. 'Where'd you think they keep their money?'

She clucked. 'I don't even *want* to think about it.'

Pete was within flicking distance of the four great shiny mounds divided by two bits of string. He stopped just short of them and started making big round shapes with his hands to make me and Angie laugh. I did, Angie didn't. But suddenly Pete stopped larking about. His hands dropped to his sides. He froze like a lolly. There was a pause while he stared at the ladies. Then he spun round and started towards us, waving his hands and making silent mouth-words we couldn't read.

'What's with him?' Angie wondered.

'What's ever with him?' I said.

While we were waiting for Pete the sunbathers turned, licking ice creams. They ducked their heads below the awning and headed back to their beach towels. They hadn't seen our faces because they didn't look our way. But we saw theirs. Oh, we saw theirs all right.

We scrambled up the beach like hot-wired rabbits. Didn't stop till we made the road. I was still in shock when I felt something prising my lips apart. I asked Angie what she thought she was doing.

'Sticking my fingers down your throat.'

I shook her off. 'Thanks, I can do it myself.'

Pete had already got his colour back. And his stupid grin. But he would, wouldn't he? It hadn't been his mother's oiled rear end he'd been queuing behind for a Mister Kreemy.

Chapter Ten

We didn't rush back to the flat. No point, bog all to do there. We strolled round Wonkton again. It wasn't the holiday town of our dreams, but at least we were a long way from school, teachers, Bryan Ryan, Eejit Atkins and the Brook Farm Estate. That didn't mean we couldn't complain, though. Some of us anyway.

'It's not exactly JoyWorld,' said Pete.

'No,' I said. 'But the sun's out.'

'Sun's probably out there too.'

'Might not be.'

'Wouldn't matter if it wasn't. Lots to do there.'

'There's one thing here that isn't at JoyWorld,' Angie said.

'What's that?' I said.

'Neville the Devil.'

'That's not a plus,' said Pete. He looked inside his pants to make sure the carrot hadn't returned.

'Would you mind not doing that when you're

with me, Garrett?' Angie said as two nearby girls ran off giggling.

'What do you think Neville wants from us?' I said.

'He told us.' Angie again. 'He wants our help to get him back to his old size.'

'He didn't say how he expects us to do it.'

'We wouldn't do it anyway,' said Pete. 'He's a menace, whatever size he is.'

'Well, we only have to keep away from that part of the beach till the end of the week,' Angie said, 'and we'll never see him again.'

'Ah, well,' I said, clearing my throat. 'He doesn't actually live on the beach.'

'No, but wherever he lives it's not likely to be near us, is it? I mean he's not exactly downstairs.'

'Glad you mentioned that, Ange.'

'Why?'

'Because...'

I told them where Neville lived.

'You mean downstairs from *us*?' said Pete.

'The flat below.'

I told them how I knew.

'Why didn't you tell us before?' Angie said.

'It sort of…didn't come up.'

'Still,' said Pete. 'There's a whole floor between us.'

I told them how Neville had come into my room last night, even though there were all those stairs. Even though the doors were closed.

Pete's teeth rattled. 'He came into your room? Our room? Last night? While we were asleep?'

'I thought he was a dream,' I said. 'He wasn't.'

'If he can come into our room whenever he wants I won't sleep a wink from now on,' Pete said.

'Great. No more snoring.'

'I don't snore.'

'Huh!'

'I do not snore!'

'How do you know if you're asleep?'

'I'd know.'

'How?'

'I'd know.'

When we'd had it with strolling we went back to the flat. The TV was on. The dads were sitting in front of it, feet on the coffee table. They wouldn't be allowed to do that at home.

'Have you been in all the time?' I asked them.

'Absolutely,' said Dad. 'Good sports channels.'

'Peg and Audrey phoned,' Oliver said.

'Don't tell me,' Angie said. 'They've been nicked for frightening the natives.'

'No, they're suggesting we take a boat out to the castle this afternoon.'

'What castle? What boat?'

'Ask them, they'll be back in a while. They're bringing some things for lunch.'

'If they're bringing things for lunch,' I said, 'they must have been to the shops.'

'Fair bet,' said Dad.

Angie looked at me in horror. The look said: 'They went like *that*?'

I drew her and Pete aside. 'If we go out with the Golden Oldies,' I said, 'we can't see the show on the beach.'

'OK by me,' said Pete.

'You'd rather spend the afternoon with the GOs than just us?'

'If it gets me out of another chinwag with that mini head-case, no contest.'

'We ought to spend *some* time with them,' Angie said. 'You know parents. Think they've failed if their kids want to be some other place all the time.'

She had a point. My mother's forehead becomes knitting when I don't fall in with her plans. She looks at me all big-eyed and tearful like I've just sold her favourite curling tongs at a car boot and I spend three days on a guilt trip.

Angie and I breathed a hefty sigh of relief when the mothers came in. They had wraparound skirt things on, so the oily goods were covered up and my breakfast stayed where it belonged. We didn't tell them we'd seen them on the beach, but Pete's grin was hard to explain. This was why, when they unpacked the shopping bags they had with them, Angie snatched a bunch of carrots and waved them in front of Pete's eyes. He went to his bunk for a lie-down.

'Look,' Mum said, 'we've caught the sun already.' She was showing off her slightly red shoulders.

'Not just there,' I muttered.

'What was that, Jiggy?'

'I said and your hair.'

'Really?'

She and Audrey battled to check their hair in the nearest mirror.

'I think he's right,' Audrey said.

'Well, it's lightened yours a bit, don't know about mine.'

'No, look, just there, I'm sure.'

'Mm...maybe.'

'I've got you a new toothbrush from the Almost Nothing shop in town,' Mum said to me and Dad when she got bored with the mirror.

'Just one?' Dad said.

She smiled and unwrapped an electric toothbrush. One.

'A Nat'n'Norman,' she said proudly.

'A who 'n' who?' I said.

'The man with the eye patch and nose ring said it's one of the most popular electric toothbrushes in North Vietnam.'

'That good, eh?' said Dad.

'*One* of the most popular,' I said. 'In case you haven't noticed, Mother, there's two of us. One is called Dad, the other's called Me.'

'That's the beauty of this,' Mum said. 'You share a handle.'

'Mum, listen,' I said, leaning closer. 'Turn up the hearing aid. It might come as a shock, but my father and I do not go to the bathroom together. And because we do not go to the bathroom together, we cannot share the handle of a single toothbrush.'

She laughed, in that twisted way she has when she thinks she's superior to all males called McCue. 'You don't have to be in the same room. You use your own *heads.*'

Dad and I looked at one another's heads. Mum laughed crazily again (the sun had obviously gone to hers) and held up a transparent packet that came with the toothbrush. The transparent packet contained an extra brush bit.

'You just slot this in and whoever didn't use the one that's already in there uses this. Two heads, one handle.'

'If you got it from an Almost Nothing shop it can't have cost much,' Dad said.

'Almost nothing,' said Mum.

'So why didn't you buy two?'

'Because there's no point in throwing money away,' she said. 'And you only have to share the handle for a week.'

I looked at Dad. Dad looked at me. We don't share stuff. Never have. It's not our way. Sharing a toothbrush handle for a week would take at least a week to get used to.

'Did you know the Romans used to whiten their teeth with urine?' Oliver said suddenly. Heads turned. 'It's true. I read it in a comic.'

'Recently?' said Dad.

'When I was a kid. It kind of stayed in my mind.'

'Did the comic also say what they polished their shoes with?'

'Not that I remember.'

'That's a relief,' said Dad.

We did the boat thing with the Golden Oldies, went to the castle with them, even smiled now and then to keep them quiet. The boat had other people in it as well as us, so we didn't say much. Couldn't have heard each other anyway over the stinky old motor. The sea was cool though. I mean nice. Really blue, like the sky. It was good to be on water, bobbing about like that. Pete didn't look too happy about the bobbing. Kept pumping his cheeks up and holding his stomach. But he could have been joking. Never can tell with Pete.

The castle was only ten minutes away. It stood on this island, just a humungous rock really. Even before the boat thumped the wooden jetty the other passengers were on their feet trying to be first off. Can you tell me why people are always in such a hurry to be first on and off things? You never see horses rushing to do that. Or fish. Well, maybe some fish. Salmon, jumping up waterfalls. But humans should know better.

When we were all off the boat we climbed this steep winding track (more uphill stuff!) to this ruin with battlements.

'Twelfth century,' Mum said when we got there.

'Looks it,' I said, puffing like a puffin.

'I bet there were some battles here.'

'Bet there were, puff-puff.'

'Imagine standing guard on those battlements on a stormy winter night.'

'Imagine. Whew, my heart.'

'Nice spot, though, isn't it?'

'Terrific.'

'You used to like castles, Jiggy.'

'I said terrific, didn't I?'

'You don't look very happy about it.'

'Don't I? Hang on.' I passed a hand over my mouth and when the hand was gone I was all teeth.

'Better?'

'Oh, Jiggy, at least *try* to enjoy yourself.'

That one's a real blister. 'At least try to enjoy yourself.' How can you try to enjoy yourself? I mean seriously, how can you try to enjoy yourself? These so-called grown-ups always say that. You either enjoy yourself or you don't enjoy yourself. If you have to try, it can't be real enjoyment, stands to reason. The Golden Oldies have been around since the dawn of time, so they should know this, but do they? No, they don't. They keep banging away with, 'Oh, do at least *try* to enjoy yourself,' like people with failed brain transplants. I worry about that generation, I really do.

Angie was quite interested in the castle, but only quite. Like me she would have enjoyed it more if it was just us three. The dads would have enjoyed it more if they weren't even there. Looked like they had trouble keeping awake as they trooped after the mothers. The mothers were the only ones who seemed to like being there, storming on ahead, running up and down steep stone staircases, looking down smelly wells and through arrow slits, reading all the little notices about the history of the dump. They even read the *'How to Use the Fire Extinguisher'* instructions.

'Didn't know they had fire extinguishers back then,' I said.

'Ho-ho-ho,' said Pete. He was the only one who didn't try to look like this was a really great day, but he perked up when the little café in the castle grounds turned out to sell Mr Kreemies. No Super-Space Fizzers though. Didn't *anyone* sell them in this lousy part of the world?

When we caught the boat back — different boat, still loud and stinky — it returned to another part of the beach. It's the way it worked. You got on at one point and came back to another, so you'd better not have left anything at the first place because it's quite a trek along the beach from the second. But that wasn't what bugged Pete.

'Of all the bits of beach in all the world,' he groaned, 'we have to come to this one.'

'Oh, look,' said my mum. 'A Punch and Judy show!'

'Don't believe everything you see,' I said.

She didn't pay any attention. Of course she didn't, she's a mother.

'Let's go and see,' said Audrey. Another one.

'Let's not,' said Pete.

But the mums were off, sprinting across the beach towards the booth. The dads weren't keen, but they followed, not sprinting, shoulders sloping wearily. Angie, Pete and I took up what's called the rear, but stopped when we reached the back of the booth. We couldn't see the show from there, of course, but we could see the bored faces of the ten or twelve kids sitting cross-legged on the sand and pebbles staring up at the stage like they had iron bars in their necks. There were some adults too, but they were watching from a distance so they wouldn't have to pay. We might not be able to see the show from where we were but we could hear it. The squeaky little voices of Neville and a female puppet which had to be Judy.

'Oh, Mr Nicey-Nicey, how good you are to poor little me.'

'It's my job, Madam. It's what I do — be good to people.'

'There's a Special Place in Heaven for people like

you, you wonderful man.'

'Kind of you to say so, Ms Sweet. Pass the baby, do.'

'What do you want the baby for, Mr Nicey-Nicey?'

'I want to cuddle it, and kiss it, and rock it in my nice arms.'

'Oh, Mr Nicey-Nicey, you are someone we should all look up to, even if you are quite small.'

'Why, thank you, Sweetheart. I will treasure your words as long as I live.'

Then, while Pete and I were bending over pretending to heave into the sand, a tinny fanfare told the audience that the show was over. There was a patter of applause from bored little hands and the audience got up brushing sand from their bored little behinds.

The dads came back first. They looked puzzled.

'I thought they bashed one another about in these things,' Oliver was saying.

'I thought they threw the baby out and someone got eaten by a crocodile or ended up swinging from a rope,' said my father.

'That was the good old days,' said another voice.

Professor Shanks stepped from the back of the booth, which he'd just unzipped from inside.

'Things have changed, have they?' Dad said to the Prof.

'Beyond sanity,' he said. 'We are now a violence-free zone, by order. My father and grandfather ran Punch and Judy on this beach for over sixty years between them. No end of thumping and shouting and good clean smacking then, with Mr Punch getting his come-uppance in the end. The kids loved it. Not now. Now they have to watch pap like this, in which no one gets hurt, no one is unkind, no one even gets very angry. I'm seriously thinking of giving it up.'

'What would you do instead?' asked Angie.

He glanced at her. 'Don't I know you?' He noticed Pete and me as well. 'Oh, you three.'

The mothers had just come round the corner of the booth.

'Have they been causing trouble?' Mum said.

'Far from it,' said the Prof. 'They helped me out earlier. Watched the booth while I went back for something I'd forgotten.'

Mum's eyebrows lifted. 'For free?'

'I invited them to watch the show gratis. Not that I blame them if they don't want to. I wouldn't want to see garbage like this.'

'You didn't say what you'd do if you gave it up,' Angie said.

'I have a business in town which I neglect,' said the Professor. 'I'll concentrate on that instead. I've only kept the show going this long because it's been in the family for three generations.'

'Need a hand with your stuff?' Angie again.

He looked pleased. 'Wouldn't say no. I have to dismantle the tent and carry it and all the gear up to the van. Means several trips for me alone.'

'OK.'

'That all right with you?' the Prof asked the Golden Oldies. The mothers said it was and started along the beach with the dads and one other.

'Garrett, get back here!' said Angie. Oliver and his son turned. 'I mean Pete,' she added.

Pete came back, kicking pebbles. He knows who's boss but he doesn't have to like it.

The booth had to be folded away, but first all the equipment had to be brought out and put in the bags and boxes the Professor kept inside during the

128

shows. There was so much stuff I don't know how he found the space to move in there. Just as well he did the entire show himself. The equipment included the puppets and the puppets included Neville and Judy. When the Professor put them away in their separate coffin-shaped boxes you would never have known one of them was alive. Neville didn't move a muscle. He didn't blink, just stared straight ahead of him, except once when he caught my eye. Then he snapped right back to staring ahead again. He was still staring when the Professor put the lid on his box.

'Can we have Mithter Nithey-Nithey's autograph?'

Two little boys who had to be twins stood there holding out an empty crisp packet, a corner each.

The Professor stopped what he was doing.

'Mr Nicey-Nicey is a puppet,' he told them.

'Yeth, but could we have hith autograph?'

'Puppet means he's not real.'

'Yeth, but could we have hith autograph?'

'His pen won't write on that.'

'Yeth, but could we have hith autograph?'

The Professor took the crisp packet. 'Hang on a tick.'

He ducked into the booth. Twenty seconds later he backed out again and handed the kids the crisp packet. They looked at it.

'Where'th hith autograph?'

The Professor pointed at the middle of the packet.

'Right there.'

The little boys bent their twin heads over the packet.

'Can't thee it.'

'It's special ink,' the Prof said. 'Mr Nicey-Nicey ink. Invisible.'

The kids looked up. Their eyes were like gobstoppers.

'Invithible?'

'Yes. It's secret ink. He only uses it for very special people.'

'Ooh. Cool.'

They turned and ran up the beach to their parents, waving the crithp packet.

'Kids,' said Professor Shanks.

The material of the booth had to be taken off the frame that made it the shape it was and folded carefully so it wouldn't crease, then the frame was taken apart and put in canvas sacks.

'I'll take these to the van,' the Prof said, hoisting the tent and frame on to his shoulder and tucking the Mr Nicey-Nicey and Ms Sweet board from the top of the booth under his arm. 'If you gather the rest together and bring the puppet boxes that would be a big help.' He started up the beach towards the road.

'Would you mind not volunteering me for stuff?' Pete said to Angie as we got to work.

'Oh, you don't like to do anything for *anyone*,' she said.

'It's his show, let him clear it away.'

'Miserable oik,' a small voice said from one of the puppet boxes.

I flipped Neville's lid. He lay on a bed of soft shiny material. If he'd had the pointy side teeth and been in neck-to-toe black instead of a yellow waistcoat and little red bowler, and if he'd been thinner, he'd have looked like a model Dracula.

'You are speaking to us then,' I said.

'That slipped out. I can't be caught talking. It's in my contract.'

'Contract?'

'If I do three shows a day, weather permitting, the Prof feeds me and puts a lid over my head, but I had to sign a contract promising to pretend I was a woodentop at all times with anyone but him. Now what do you say we move this along a little? Like get down to the reason I brought you to Wonkton and how you can get me my size back.'

'You didn't bring us here,' Pete said. 'You had nothing to do with us coming here. We missed our plane, that's all. We were going somewhere else entirely till then.'

'To JoyWorld,' said Neville.

'How did you know about us going to JoyWorld?'

He tapped the rim of his bowler. 'I'm a little devil.'

'Nev?' said a voice from another box. 'Nev, who you talking to?'

'Not you, windbag,' he said. 'Get on your pogo stick and hop off.'

Angie opened the box the second voice came from. Little Judy blinked at the light.

'I'll tell the Professor,' she said, lifting her head. 'You've been talking to people. You're not supposed to talk to people. He's not supposed to talk to people,' she said to us.

'Shut her lid,' Neville said.

Judy sat up. 'I'll shut your lid, you bully, for good and all I will.'

'We thought it was just you who was real,' I said to Neville in amazement.

'It was,' he said. 'Till I made the mistake of devilling her.'

'Devilling her?'

'It was raining. The Prof had gone to his shop and I was stuck in that crummy flat all by myself, bored out of my bowler. I needed someone to chat to, so…'

'You brought Judy to life,' said Angie.

'I was better off before,' Judy said. 'Didn't need to eat then.'

'You wouldn't eat now if not for me,' Neville said. 'Don't I share my chow with you?'

'There's never enough. I'm half-starved. The Professor would feed me if he knew I was alive.'

'He's depressed enough already without laying that on him. Do you have any idea how much power I wasted bringing you to life? That's power

133

I'll never get back. How about some gratitude here?'

He kicked her box. Judy squawked and fell back. The lid came down on her. She went quiet. Neville turned to us.

'Seeing as you've come all this way to help me,' he said, 'there's a little extra something you could do for me while you're at it.'

'What's that?' Angie said.

'Throw the crone under a bus for me.'

Chapter Eleven

It was while we were loading the last of the Professor's things on to the van that we noticed that the Three Musketeers were down to two.*

'Where's Pete?' I said.

'Who?' said the Prof.

'He was here a minute ago. Must have bunked off.'

'Wait till I see him,' Angie said.

When we'd finished loading up we left the Professor and wandered off. We had some talking to do.

'There's a lot I don't get about all this,' Angie said.

'Like?' I said.

'Like Neville saying he brought us here. He didn't. The ancient hippy at the airport took pity on us and gave us the keys to the holiday flat he couldn't use. Nothing to do with Neville.'

'Maybe the whole thing's a set-up.'

---

* In case you haven't heard, Angie, Pete and I call ourselves the Three Musketeers. That's because there are three of us. Clever, eh? We're a secret society, so keep it to yourself or we'll come after you. Well, Angie will.

'A set-up?'

'Maybe Neville *sent* the ancient hippy.'

'How could Neville send anyone? He's puppet-sized.'

'I don't know. But think about it. How likely is it that the ancient hippy would give us the keys to the flat just upstairs from him – from Neville, the only person in Wonkton we've met before?'

'Yes,' Angie said. 'But even a little devil like him couldn't know we were going to miss the plane.'

'Perhaps he made us miss it.'

'How could he do that?'

'Don't know that either. But the hairy hippy seemed kind of edgy, I thought. Nervous. If he'd been playing it straight he wouldn't have… Woh!'

'What?'

'Super-Space Fizzers.'

We'd wandered into the main shopping street and were passing this little ice cream kiosk with a board in the window which had a pic of a Super-Space Fizzer that wasn't faded like the one at the beach.

'Do you sell Super-Space Fizzers?' I asked the girl filing her nails in the kiosk.

'Is there a picture of one?' she asked, not looking up.

'Yes, but do you sell them?'

'If we didn't, there wouldn't be a picture.'

My heart leapt. I grabbed my pocket. Dipped in it for the money. I was actually going to get a Super-Space Fizzer!

'Can I have one?'

The girl tutted, sighed like a water-buffalo, stuck her nail file in her hair, and lifted the lid of the freezer behind her. Then she dropped the freezer lid and slumped back in her seat.

'None left.'

'What?'

'All gone.'

'All gone?'

'Ain't got none.'

'Ain't got none?'

'We're out.'

We went on our way.

'I wonder,' Angie said.

'Wonder what?'

'If Neville did make us miss our plane. To do that he would've had to make us late. And we were late.

And why were we late?'

'Because my dad couldn't get off the fruit machines at the motorway service station.'

'I was thinking of the airport car park signs. We all thought the same. That they were pointing a different way the first time. Well suppose they were? Suppose someone switched them to make us go the wrong way and be late, and the ancient hippy was just waiting to pounce with the keys?'

We came to the shop that Pete had been so fascinated by. Striker's Magic Joke Shop. I pointed to The Combo Fun Box that he'd drooled over.

'Think Pete'll buy that?'

'If he can't wangle the money out of his dad,' Angie said, 'he'll go on and on and on about it all week until in the end we'll go thirds with him to get some peace.'

'Don't count on a third from me,' I said.

'You'll weaken. No one can hold out against Pete when he won't let something go.'

We moved off down the street.

'If Neville switched the signs and all the rest of it,' I said, 'that means he really did get us here because he needs our help to get his size back for him.'

'Which we're not going to do,' Angie said. 'He's not safe his normal size.'

'He's not safe *this* size if he can make us miss car parks and planes and come to Wonkton-on-Sea. And look what he did to Pete. More size might mean more power, and if he has more power who knows what he might do to the rest of the world.'

'That's why we can't help him,' Angie said. 'Why we mustn't.'

'I wasn't planning to,' I said. 'There's nothing he can do that would make me help him.'

'Even if he turned parts of you into carrots?'

'Even if he turned parts of me into cucumbers.'

'What about string beans?'

'Even then.'

'Bananas?'

'Nope.'

'Plums, pineapples, Cox's Pippins?'

'No, no, no.'

'Seedless raisins?'

'It wouldn't matter what,' I said. 'The spell he laid on Pete didn't last, did it? All I'd have to do would be to sit tight until I stopped looking like a human fruit and veg stall. I can do that.'

It wasn't until teatime that we started to miss Pete. I don't mean miss him exactly. You don't miss Pete, you just notice he's not there. The dads had gone out for takeaways and the mothers asked us to lay the table while they talked about hair or eye-shadow or something.

'Do we have to eat at the table?' Angie said. 'We're on holiday.'

'Where would you suggest if not the table?' said her mum.

'In chairs. Front of the telly.'

'There's nothing on at this time. We don't want to watch just anything because we're on holiday – do we, Peg?'

'No, we don't,' my mother said firmly.

Those two. They should have their own dictatorship.

'Pete better get a move on if he wants to eat,' Angie said to me.

'More for us if he's late,' I said, starting to lay the table.

'He might have lost track of time. I'll text him.' Angie got to work on her mobile. Pause. Then she said: 'It won't go. I'm getting a "Not Sent" message.'

'Probably a bad signal. Try it from somewhere else.'

She went to the other side of the room while I finished the table. Seven places, but there were only six chairs. Typical.

'Still nothing,' Angie said.

'Lean out of the window. Good view. I speak from experience. We're a chair short.'

'There's a couple of stools in the kitchen,' she said, going to the window.

I went to the kitchen for one of the stools. It was way too low, but it didn't really matter because I wasn't planning to sit on it.

'No dice,' Angie said, pulling back from the window. 'Well, I tried.'

'He'll be here,' I said. 'You know Pete. Won't miss his nosh.'

When the dads came in with bags full of curry, the mothers started putting it on plates in the kitchen.

'Why don't we just put all the containers in the middle of the table and dip in as we feel like it?' Dad said.

'Because we're civilised human beings,' my mother replied.

'Speak for yourself.'

But he sat down at the table with me, Angie and Oliver to wait for the hot stuff and rice.

'Maths never was your strong point, was it, Jig?' Dad said.

'Sorry?'

'Unless you've got an imaginary friend…'

I didn't get it. Nor did Angie. I twisted a finger to my head.

Mum and Audrey came in with the first four plates.

'Open the wine, Oll,' Audrey said.

'Me and Mel don't want wine,' he said. 'We've got beer.'

'Well open it for *us*, please.'

Oliver tried to get the corkscrew to work while the women went back to the kitchen for the other plates. When they returned they sat down – not on the stool.

'Give me that!' Audrey said, snatching the corkscrew and bottle from Oliver. 'I really don't know what's so hard about opening a bottle. You never can do it.'

'Screw goes the wrong way,' he said.

'Only for a person of below average intelligence.'

'They ought to put press tops on wine bottles,' said my dad. 'They put them on beer cans, why not wine bottles? A child could open them then.'

'And easy access to wine for children would be good, would it?' Mum said.

'Figure of speech,' said Dad.

They dipped their forks into their food. Angie and I hadn't started yet because we'd been taught from the cradle that if we start before everyone else our fingers are served up in the next Chinese.

'You left some for Pete, didn't you?' Angie said.

Audrey and my mother looked puzzled.

'Pete? Remember him?' said Ange.

They went right on looking puzzled.

'Jig laid an extra place,' Oliver said with a wink.

The mothers noticed the extra place and the stool. They smiled. When Mum got up and went back to the kitchen the three remaining Golden Oldies eyed Ange and me like we were six years old.

'What?' we said, together. They just grinned.

Mum came back with another plate. A small

one, like for a little kid or for bits of gristle you might want to spit out. She put a spoonful of her curry and rice on it.

'Any other contributions?' she said.

Audrey put a spoonful of hers on the little plate.

'Oh, come *on*,' Dad said when Mum looked at him.

Oliver didn't bother either. Angie and I just didn't get it.

'What was his name again?' Mum said to us. 'Paul? Here we are then, Paul. Eat it up like a good boy.'

Suddenly we understood. Or thought we did. The GOs were having us on. Once we realised this we went along with it.

'Tuck it away, Paul,' Angie said.

'Get stuck in there, boy.' This was me.

'Boy?' Audrey said. 'Oh, he's a dog.'

'Dog?' I said. 'No, he's a boy. That's why I said, "Get stuck in there, boy". If he was a dog I'd say, "Get stuck in there, dog".'

'No, you'd probably still say boy,' Angie said.

'I wouldn't.'

'You would. Everyone does.'

'I don't, and you know why? Because I haven't got a dog.'

'You've got a kennel.'

'Doesn't make me a dog-owner. And that kennel wasn't meant for a dog. Wasn't meant for anything, it was a woodwork project.'*

'I know, but if you made a kennel when you could have made absolutely anything – a candlestick, say, or a domino – I reckon you secretly wanted a dog and hoped someone would get you one.'

'Wrong,' I said. 'I never wanted a dog. I don't like dogs. I wouldn't have a dog if it was shredded and spiced and put in a curry.'

The Golden Oldies stopped eating and looked at their plates like they hadn't noticed them before but Ange and I tucked in. We were still tucking when we heard the main door bang downstairs.

'Must be him,' Angie said.

We'd started leaving the downstairs door unlocked when anyone was out so they could get back in without ringing or knocking.

'Must be who?' my mother asked.

'Pete.'

'Pete? Another imaginary friend?'

---

* The kennel woodwork project happens in *Maggot Pie*.

'No, same one.'

'I thought his name was Paul and he was already here.'

Every eye but Angie's and mine looked at the empty stool. Angie's eyes and my eyes looked at one another's. Why were these people acting so weird? Was it the sea air? Still, Pete would be halfway up the stairs by now. Any second he'd be kicking the door to be let in, then we could get back to normal.

But Pete didn't kick the door to be let in. The door we'd heard must have been the Professor going out. Pete wasn't mentioned again until after tea when Angie asked Oliver if he had any idea where Pete had got to. 'Pete?' Ollie said. 'Are you still playing that?'

Angie took me aside. 'Is there something going on here that we don't know about?'

'If there is,' I said, 'we don't know about it.'

'No one seems bothered that Pete hasn't come back.'

'No one seems to *remember* him,' I said.

'What are they playing at?'

'I don't know, but a joke's a joke.'

'It's beyond a joke. Let's get out of here.'

We told the Golden Oldies we were going and the mothers said, 'Don't get into trouble,' 'Watch the roads,' 'Don't talk to strangers,' and we said, 'Yeah, yeah,' and went.

Passing the door downstairs we heard tiny voices – Neville and Judy's – arguing.

'He deserves all he gets,' I whispered as we carried on down.

Angie's mobile worked once we were away from Journey's End, but when she tried Pete again she still couldn't connect. We looked all over town for him. Walked every street, looked down every alley, in every doorway, went to the beach, everywhere we could think of. Angie tried his number every ten minutes or so. Still no connection. The phone thing didn't make sense. Pete never turned his phone off, and he made sure the batteries never ran down and that he always had credit. It was as if his phone had stopped existing. Like him.

'Maybe he went back to the flat by another route and arrived just after we left,' I said. 'You can't get a signal in the flat, so that's why we still can't reach him.'

'That doesn't explain why the GOs couldn't remember him.'

'They were kidding. Pulling our proverbials.'

'Mm...' She didn't sound too sure. 'I'll phone my mum to see if he's there.'

'Won't be able to get through,' I said.

'I'll try anyway.'

She fingered Audrey's number and listened. Nothing. Then Oliver's. Even less.

'Could be why it's called Journey's End,' I said. 'Dead signal area. Last stop for all who stay there. We'll disappear one by one and each time one of us goes the rest won't be able to remember them, and by the end of the week there'll only be one of us left, which'll be me, and I'll think I came on holiday by myself because I'm an only child, then on Saturday morning even I won't be there.'

We started up the hill. After a few steps I was wheezing a bit, but I couldn't stop the thoughts coming now that I was on a roll.

'Suppose it's just Pete,' I said.

'Just Pete?'

'Who's going to disappear. When you think about it, we're always wishing he would. We say

"Disappear, Garrett" ten times a day. Eleven on Sundays.'

'Only because he's always saying stupid things and telling stupid jokes. We don't mean it. Not seriously. Not really.'

'Maybe not, but we've said it so often that we could have reached just the right...sheez, this hill...number.'

'Right number?'

'Yes, like...like maybe if you wish for something enough times – six hundred and thirteen, say – it happens. Remember the genie? Not wishes exactly but the same sort of thing.* We might have said, "Disappear, Garrett" six hundred and thirteen times, the magic number that...whew!...gets people zapped. No more Pete, even in people's memories.'

'He's still in our memories.'

'That's because we were the ones who disappeared him.'

'Shut up, Jig, you're spooking me.'

I shut up, mainly because I had to. That hill was too steep to climb *and* talk. When we reached the top I leant against the wall, gulping like a goldfish.

---

* *Maggot Pie* again. Read all about the Piddle Pool Genie there.

Angie wasn't out of breath at all. She only gets a breath shortage if she runs really hard. Pete gets it after two metres, going downhill.

Pete. What if I was right about him? What if he really had vanished from the face of the earth? Who would I sit next to in class?

Chapter Twelve

Angie went up first. I followed a step at a time because my legs were on a go-slow. I was still only halfway when she reached the top of the stairs and went into our flat. I slithered down the wall outside the Professor's door for a rest.

'Why don't you come in?' said a squeaky little voice.

'I'm all right here,' I answered.

'There's stuff you need to know,' Neville said.

'Where's the Professor?'

'He's out. Travolta Night at the Hog's Head. He's been practicing his Seventies Strut for weeks.'

Then there was another voice – Judy's, grumbling – and Neville's again, telling her to can it. I hauled myself up and opened the door. I went in. Neville sat on the sofa. Judy was sitting up in her box. They were watching a makeover show on the TV, but you could hardly hear it.

'I said I don't want visitors,' Judy snapped. 'I'm watching this programme. Not that I can hear it with the sound so low.'

'The sound's low so we can hear Shanks if he comes back early,' Neville said. 'You want him to catch you sitting up watching TV? Take a pew,' he said to me.

'I don't want to hang around here,' I said, not taking a pew. 'Just tell me what you think I should know.'

'Relax. He'll be gone for hours. Sit.'

I parked myself in the armchair opposite him. He looked so small on that sofa, mainly because he was. There could have been ten his size sitting there, side by side by side. He wasn't wearing his little hat for a change, but small as he was, there was nothing cute about him. Nothing at all.

'OK, get it over with.'

'Get it over with?' he said. 'Is that all you want? I thought you'd be full of questions.'

'What questions?'

'Questions like how I knew you were going on holiday. Like how I got you all the way to Wonkton-on-Sea when you were heading for somewhere else entirely. Don't you want to know these things?'

He was so keen to show off, tell me how clever he was, that I said, 'Couldn't care less,' even though it wasn't true.

He looked a bit disappointed, but tried to cover it up. 'It's your loss. But before we go any further let me repeat, in case you missed it so far, that I want my size back and you're going to help me get it back.'

'Oh. Am I?'

'Yes. You are. And when I get it back I'm out of here, el pronto.'

'I know you want to leave me,' Judy said. 'You don't have to pretend.'

Neville shot her a killer glance. 'Who's pretending? Of course I want to leave you, spud-head. You have a bad personality, you never stop nagging, and you're about as beautiful as an old elephant's backside. Who wouldn't want to leave you?'

'You must have liked me once or you wouldn't have brought me to life,' she replied weepily.

'Don't flatter yourself. The only other puppets

around were the baby, the crocodile and the dude in blue. If I'd known then what I know now I'd have gone for the croc.'

Judy's face crumpled like a used tissue. Tears spat from her eyes.

'Oh, Neville, how can you treat me this way!'

'Easy as burping,' said Nev. 'Put a stopper in it, I wanna talk to my friend here.' He turned back to me. 'I'll put it in plain English in case it ain't sunk in yet. You made me like this so you got to put me right. That's the way it works. The one that does unto one is the one that must undo one. Ancient devilric scripture.'

'Why should I help you?' I said. 'You never did me any favours. You did me the opposite of favours.'

He laid his big insincere grin on me. 'I didn't know you then.'

'You don't know me now.'

'Sure I do. We're neighbours. You're the brat from…you're the nice young man from upstairs.'

'Keep the noise down,' Judy said. 'I can't hear my programme.'

'Keep *your* noise down,' said Nev. 'We're talking business here.'

'Well if you can't talk in whispers move me closer to the TV.'

'Hey kid, move the crone, willya?'

I got up and went to Judy's box.

'You be careful now, boy,' Judy said, gripping the sides.

'I'll be careful.'

I lifted her box and put it on a small table in front of the telly.

'Not this close!' Judy screeched. 'It's bad for a person's eyes to be this close to the screen.'

'How do you know that if you've been a puppet all your life?' I asked, pulling the table back a bit.

She looked up at me with a smile like a bent hairpin. 'I'm old. I have wisdom.'

'You're just old,' Neville growled. 'What's your tab, kid?' he said to me as I sat down again.

'My tab?'

'Your label, your moniker, your handle.'

'Um, Jiggy,' I said.

'Um-Jiggy?'

'Jiggy.'

'That's your *name*?'

'It's what I answer to.'

'Kinda stupid, isn't it?'

'I'm really sorry you don't like it.'

'No, no, I love it. I never heard such a terrific name. Best name I've heard since Hepsibah Eustacia Bluebell Trott.'

'Who?'

'Panto dame I met a while back. Look, kid...Twiggy?'

'Jiggy.'

'Jiggy. Right. It doesn't get any better just by saying it a few times, but listen...Jiggy...the reason you should help me is that you're a really warm, generous human being.'

'You don't know that.'

'Sure I do. I'm a terrific judge of handsome young human types.'

'And *how* would I help you?'

'By going to a certain place not so far from here and bringing back the one thing that'll give me some size.'

'What place, what thing?'

'I can't tell you the place. If I told you where to go, something terrible would happen to me.'

'What sort of something?'

He squirmed. 'I'd become…un-devilish.'

'You mean you'd lose your powers?'

'Every last one. I'd be as useless as you.'

'Sounds good to me,' I said. 'Without the powers you wouldn't be able to cause any more mischief.'

'Mischief's my business,' he said. 'It's what I do. Without the mischief I might as well be a newsagent. But if you help me get my size back I'll have myself a ball. I didn't do much last time. I was just learning the ropes then. Next time…oh boy, just watch me!'

'You seriously think I'd help you become an even greater pest?'

'Well, I was kinda hoping.'

'I wouldn't help you, Mr Nicey-Nicey, if you were the last little devil in Wonkton.'

'What do you mean the last?' he said. 'I'm the *only* little devil in Wonkton. So is that a no? You won't do the decent thing?'

'No. Absolutely not.'

'You might want to rethink that, kiddo. Remember your friend.'

'You mean the fruit and veg stunt?'

'I could do the same to you, no problem.'

'I'd be ready for you. Even with carrots for fingers I could grab you and stick your head in the stinkiest public toilet I could find.'

'You couldn't if I turned you into a cactus.'

'Then I'd prick you.'

'Or a cat.'

'I'd claw you.'

'A rat?'

'I'd gnaw you.'

'A bee. I could turn you into a bee. How would you like that?'

'Where would you like to be stung first?'

'You couldn't do much as a moth,' Neville said. 'If I turned you into a moth I could catch you and squash you.'

'I'd fly out of your reach.'

'I'd dinkoon a long-handled moth net.'

'I'd fly higher.'

'A super-long-handled moth net.'

'Be too heavy for you. I bet you can't dinkoon yourself some extra strength. And I'd flutter in your face all night while you were trying to sleep.'

'You couldn't,' he said with a superior smirk. 'None of the spells I can do while this size last more than a few minutes.'

'I wouldn't have long to worry about it then, would I?'

He screwed his smirk up and threw it away. He'd just admitted his big weakness. I mean his little weakness.

'Jig? That you?'

Angie's voice, outside the door, followed by some knuckles.

'In here.'

She stuck her head in. 'What's going on?'

'Mr Nicey-Nicey is telling me what he'll do to me if I don't help him.'

'Bad things?'

'Sad things.'

'Where's the Professor?'

'Out.'

She came in. 'The Golden Oldies weren't pulling a fast one,' she said. 'They really don't remember Pete. Far as they're concerned he never existed. But I went in your room and his pyjamas are still in a knot under his pillow where he left them, and his case is still under your bunk. Anything he brought with him is still there, but the GOs think they're yours or mine.'

'I don't get it,' I said.

'It's him,' said Judy from the table in front of the TV.

'What's who?' Angie asked.

'The little devil with the bag of chips on his shoulder. He's been misbehaving.'

'What does she mean?' I asked Neville.

'It's called leverage,' he said.

'Leverage?'

'Something you use to make people do what you want.'

'What's this to do with Pete?'

'Pete? Was that his name?'

'Pete *is* his name,' Angie said, squatting in front of Neville. 'Is there something you know that we don't?'

Neville laughed a devilish laugh.

'You could say that.'

Angie gripped him by the shoulders. The devilish laugh became a squeak as she squeezed.

'What do you know about Pete's disappearance?'

'You're hurting me,' said Neville.

'Squeeze harder,' said Judy.

'Tell me,' said Angie.

'If you don't let go I'll turn you into something nasty.'

'If you turn her into something,' I said, 'you'll be out the window before you can even think of turning me into something too.'

'All right, I'll tell you,' he said, 'just let go of me.' Angie let go of him. He tugged his waistcoat down. 'I woulda told you anyway. There's no point having leverage if the leveree doesn't know about it.'

'OK, spill the beans,' I said.

'Why would I do that?' said Neville.

'It means tell us everything.'

'What kind of beans?'

'It doesn't matter what kind, just beans.'

'I don't like all beans. I *hate* baked beans.'

'Never mind what kind of beans.'

'Broad beans too.'

'Forget the beans.'

'And you can keep French beans, cannelloni beans and soya beans. And kidney beans. Can't see the point of kidney beans.'

'I don't like kidney beans either,' Angie said. 'Except in chilli.'

'Don't you start,' I said.

'Quite fond of bean *sprouts*, though,' Neville said.

'They don't count,' said Ange.

'Butter beans count. I'm partial to the odd butter bean.'

'I'm going to lose it in a minute,' I said.

'And there's always borlotti beans,' said Neville.

'I don't think I've ever had borlotti beans,' Angie said.

'Me neither. We oughtta give 'em a try sometime.'

'Have we finished with the beans?' I said.

'You were the one that wanted me to spill them,' said Neville.

'I'm hungry now,' said Judy from her box.

'So go for a takeaway and forget to come back,' said Neville.

'Oh, you're so *horrible* to me,' she wailed.

'I'll try,' he said.

'What do you know about Pete's disappearance?' I asked him.

'And our folks not remembering him,' said Angie.

'He knows everything,' said Judy through her sobs.

I leaned towards Neville. 'You're responsible?'

'Who else?' he said. 'I knew you wouldn't help me without some sort of incentive, so I took one of your friends.'

'You took Pete?' said Angie. Neville smiled.

'How do you mean...took him?' I said.

'Don't worry, no one'll miss him. He's been erased from every memory except yours. If he has other friends, they no longer remember him. Nor do his neighbours or teachers back home.'

I knew some teachers who wouldn't complain about that if they knew, but I didn't say so.

'What have you done with him?' Angie demanded.

'I removed him from existence,' Neville said.

'You what?'

'Put him out of circulation till you solve my little problem.'

'You haven't hurt him?'

'No, he's fine. But...'

He grinned horribly at us, one after the other.

'But we don't get him back unless we do what you want,' I said.

'That's the deal, Biggy.'

'Jiggy.'

'Jig, we must do what he asks,' Angie said. 'For Pete's sake.'

Neville laughed. 'For Pete's sake. Good one.'

'Looks like you win then,' I said. 'We have no choice but to help you become a full-sized menace to society.'

Neville clapped his little hands. 'I knew you'd see it my way.'

Chapter Thirteen

We didn't stay long downstairs because the Professor came back sooner than expected. But before that happened I told Angie about the thing we were supposed to find that would cure Neville of his smallness and the place we'd find it, which he couldn't name because he'd lose his devilishness. Angie being Angie, she immediately started quizzing him.

'When you say this place isn't far from here,' she said, 'how near do you mean?'

He shook his head. 'I can't go into details.'

'Like is it in Wonkton, or just outside Wonkton, or where? Which direction? And is it a house, a village, a phone box…what?'

'Can't say.'

'You must be able to give us some clue,' she said.

'Nope. Not even a tiny one. Except…'

'Except?'

'Except that it's where I'm from. In a manner of

speaking. Where I...came into the world.'

'But that could be anywhere,' I said.

Neville narrowed his little eyes at me. 'Use your imagination, Ziggy. You got one of those, or have you grown out of it already, like most human males?'

'Jiggy,' I said.

'Jiggy's got more imagination than's good for him,' Angie said.

'So get him to use it. And bring yours out of retirement too while you're at it. Two feeble human imaginations might just manage to work this thing out. It's not micro-technology, it's not particle physics, it's observation and common sense. And sense doesn't get more common than the human kind.'

'You don't think much of us, do you?' I said.

'You're an inferior species. What do you expect, a pat on the back for learning how to button a shirt?'

'OK,' Angie said. 'So somehow we work out where this place is. Then what? What's this cure we have to find?'

'It's not a cure as such,' said Neville. 'It's...an instrument.'

'You play it?' I said.

He rolled his eyes like mini-marbles. 'No, you don't play it. It's a tool. A tool used by devils the world over. A trident.'

'What's a trident?'

'What's a trident? Don't they teach you kids anything these days?'

'They teach,' said Angie. 'It's just that some of us, like this one, don't pay attention. Paying attention's against their religion.'

'Don't talk to me about religion,' said Neville the Devil.

'I wasn't going to. A trident,' she said to me, 'is a long fork sort of thing with three prongs on the end.'

'Usually red,' said Neville. 'My prongs are red.'

'Why can't you fetch it yourself?' I asked.

'Why? Because of who I am, of course.'

'Who you are?'

'I'm supposed to be a puppet. If I was seen walking the streets like this the Tabloids'd be all over Wonkton in fifteen minutes. And there's the size thing. It takes me two days to jog half a mile. No, you have to find the place and get the trident that'll make me big and powerful again. Your task for the week, kiddos.'

'And when you get it back,' Angie said, 'what then?'

'Then I realise my full potential. I didn't make the most of my powers last time. I wanted to be a devil with a difference. A businessman devil. I thought that a businessman wouldn't go round swishing his tail and threatening terrible things.'

'A businessman?' I said. 'You ran a market stall.'

'I was learning the ropes, flexing my horns. If you hadn't come along and ruined everything I'd be on the cover of *Goodbye* magazine by now. Maybe even a *Playfiend* centrefold.'

'Do you actually have a tail?' Angie asked.

'Sure I do,' he said. He waggled his eyebrows. 'Wanna see it?'

I don't know what her reply would have been because that was when we heard the Prof come in downstairs. Nev went all panicky.

'He's back already! Hey, crone, lie down!' he said to Judy. 'Put her lid on, willya?' he said to me.

Judy fell back in her box and I dropped her lid. Then I ran after Angie, who was already on the landing. I closed the door, very quietly. The Professor was on the stairs but he didn't look up, didn't see us. He was decked out in this sharp white suit and jerking his shoulders and hips in this very peculiar way, and singing something about 'staying alive' in this very high voice.

The flat upstairs, our unrented holiday flat, felt strange now. It looked normal enough, sounded it, but it wasn't, because of what me and Angie knew and the Golden Oldies didn't. The dads were watching more sport (don't they ever get *enough*?) and Mum and Audrey were sitting as far away from them as they could, nattering quietly. None of them had any idea we were one missing. Oliver didn't know he was a father and that back home on the Brook Farm Estate he shared a house with his son as well as with Aud and Ange. How could he not know that? How could Audrey not know it? How could their best friends, my parents, not know it?

'The wanderers return!' my mother said as we went in.

She's always saying stuff like this, my mum. Things people have been saying for centuries,

Dad says. He calls them old chestnuts. Here are some of the old chestnuts my mother says all the time.

All things come to those who wait.

No news is good news.

You live and learn.

You'll survive, Jiggy.

Life is what you make it.

C'est la vie.

Tomorrow is another day.

Nothing's for free, Jiggy.

That's all the thanks I get.

It's always darkest before the dawn.

I have eyes in the back of my head.*

Haste makes waste.

Cheer up, it's not the end of the world.

I'm only human, Mel.

I'm not shouting. THIS IS SHOUTING!

You can't have it all ways, Jiggy.

If you can't beat 'em, join 'em.

Eat those crusts, they're good for you.

Beauty is in the eye of the beholder.

You can't tell a book by its cover.

It'll feel better when it stops hurting, Jiggy.

---

* You should see her in glasses!

Worse things happen at sea.

Life goes on.

When it rains, it pours.

Well at least I *tried*, Mel.

Must you watch this rubbish, Jiggy?

No point crying over spilt milk.

We're going to the dogs.

It's on the tip of my tongue.

Early to bed, early to rise.

I wait on you two hand and foot.

Rome wasn't built in a day, Jiggy.

It's a sign of the times.

You're your own worst enemy, Mel.

You can't make a silk purse out of a sow's ear.

Jiggy, that will make you go blind.

Every cloud has a silver lining.

I am *this* close to losing it.

Oh, sod it. (One of Dad's.)

When we went into the flat and my mother said, 'The wanderers return!' Angie and I decided after a split second's eye contact to see if we could jog their memories a bit.

'We've been looking for Pete,' Angie said.

'Still looking for him, eh?' said Oliver.

'Yes, still looking for your one and only son.'

They all had a big laugh about that.

'You two and your imaginary friend,' said Audrey.

'I thought it was Steve,' said Dad.

'Paul,' said Mum.

'No, it was Steve, wasn't it?' Dad said to us.

'No,' we said together.

'Paul, wasn't it?' said Mum.

'No. And we don't have an imaginary friend.'

'Well who was sitting beside you at tea?' Dad said.

'Nobody, the stool was empty, didn't you notice?'

The Golden Oldies looked at one another. They couldn't make sense of this. They have trouble keeping up at their age.

'We have stuff to do,' Angie said to me out of the side of her mouth.

'We do?' I said out of the side of mine.

'Have you forgotten the conversation we just had?'

'Which conversation?'

'The one downstairs with you-know-who.'

'What about it?'

She gripped one of my elbows and pushed it all the way to the kitchen. Fortunately the rest of me decided to go with it. She plonked me down on one of the stools.

'Neville has kidnapped Pete, right?'

'Kidnapped? Would you call it that?'

'Only because it sounds better than "removed from existence". He's kidnapped Pete and made everyone but us think he was never here.'

'Well he was only here one night,' I said.

'I mean never *anywhere*. If Pete never came back no one would miss him, so it's up to us to get him back, and the only way we can do that is to find this trident that'll return Neville to his proper size, and to do *that* we have to find the place where it's at.'

'How do we find the place it's at when we haven't the faintest idea where it is?'

'We get a local map and see if anything leaps out at us.'

'Where do we get a local map?'

'A local map shop, where'd you think?'

'Well we can't do that now, they're all shut.'

'First thing in the morning then.'

'OK. First thing in the morning.'

Later, alone in my room, I realised that I could have the top bunk and I was quite chirpy for the five and a half seconds it took me to remember that Garrett's disgusting feet had been up there and change my mind. Then I realised something else. I realised that I couldn't sleep up there anyway because it wasn't really my bunk, it was Pete's, and Pete wasn't there. He wasn't anywhere. But here's a funny thing. That kid is a pain in the bahoozah an awful lot of the time. As well as the feet and the chronic jokes, and the way he acts even more stupid than he is to annoy everyone, including the teachers, I...

No. I can't say it. You'll think I've gone soft.

Chapter Fourteen

I got to the Nat'n'Norman toothbrush before Dad the night of the day Pete disappeared. After using it I took the original brush out of the handle and put the other one in so Dad wouldn't put mine in his mouth in spite of the words 'JIG'S HEAD' printed on the stem with a felt tip.

I had an electric toothbrush once before. I liked the way you didn't have to move your hand much because the brush did the work for you. Present from my grandmother, that toothbrush. Came through the post in a padded envelope one birthday because she doesn't like to travel. The reason I stopped using my birthday brush was that you had to charge it up and the charger had to be plugged in the shaver socket over the bathroom basin but the lead wasn't very long so I had to balance the charger on one of the stupid little soap tray things on either side of the mirror and when my father went into the bathroom just after I put the brush on charge for the first time he threw the door back and the bulging dressing gowns behind the door hit the charger on the stupid little soap tray and knocked it off and the plug came out of the shaver point and the charger crashed to the floor taking the toothbrush with it and the toothbrush never worked again and I think that's the longest sentence I've written without a comma since my gran sent me the toothbrush when I was eight, wa-hey!

If you've never seen an electric toothbrush in action, you're supposed to put this little blob of toothpaste on this little round brush, and close your lips over it so it doesn't splatter everything in sight when the brush starts moving. Then you press the button on the handle and move the brush round your mouth one tooth at a time until the job's done, and then you turn it off. That's how it was with my Gran's electric toothbrush anyway, the few times I used it before my father destroyed it. The Nat 'n' Norman wasn't quite as smooth as that one. For starters, it didn't hum quietly while it worked. It gave a terrifying high-pitched whine like a chainsaw turning a forest into matchsticks.

When I turned it on and the high-pitched whine started I whipped it out in shock. Toothpaste spattered the mirror like a fistful of wet dandruff. I turned the brush off and leant against the sink while my heart got its normal rhythm back, then I put it nervously back in my mouth. The brush, I mean. I turned it on again. The whine started up and the bristles tucked into my teeth like a starving rat, shaking my head like a dustbin stacked with empty baked bean cans. When I'd finished I half expected to find that my gleaming teeth in the spattered mirror had become gleaming gums. The teeth were still there, but I wasn't sure how long they'd stand up to a brush as fierce as that.

Later I heard Dad go in the bathroom, and after a bit the terrifying whine of the brush followed by a shout and a crash. Everyone rushed to see what had happened and discovered that the Nat'n' Norman had been too much for him after a hard day hammering the beer in front of sports channels. When the high-pitched whine started he panicked, the brush jerked out of his mouth and hand, flew out the window, almost killed something flying peacefully by, and plunged to the street far below in a storm of white feathers.

'I don't get it,' Mum said to Dad from the bathroom window. 'What have electric toothbrushes ever done to you?'

'Almost nothing,' I said.

Next morning I cleaned my teeth with one of my fingers again. It wasn't the greatest finger in the world, and it wasn't electric, but at least I knew where it had been. And it didn't whine.

'Glad to see you're getting the most out of your holiday!' Mum sang as Angie and I headed for the door after breakfast.

'Not half as much as we'd've got out of JoyWorld!' I sang back.

We were passing the halfway door when it opened and Professor Shanks looked out. He was still in his pyjamas and his hair was all over the place and there were bags under his eyes. He jumped back when he saw us because he hadn't expected to find kids outside his door. Then he saw who it was.

'What are you two doing here?'

We told him we were staying in the flat upstairs

for the week, which seemed to surprise him.

'I didn't know old Woodstock rented out his flat.'

There was nothing we could say to that, partly because we didn't know who old Woodstock was.

'Having a good time?' he said next.

'Could be better,' I said.

'Great. Well, I'm just going down to fetch my milk.'

I eyed his pyjamas. 'The shop on the hill?'

'The step downstairs. I have it delivered.'

'Semi-skimmed?'

'Full cream.'

'I'll get it,' said Ange, and down the stairs she went. That girl is so helpful sometimes it's embarrassing. Specially embarrassing for me, suddenly waiting on stairs with a man in pyjamas, nothing to say.

'Here you are,' she said, coming up with a bottle of full cream.

The Prof took it and thanked her. 'Be seeing you,' he said, and closed the door.

Outside it looked like being another nice day. Nice enough for a quest anyway. That's what Angie called it. A quest. She also called it a mission.

'Make up your mind,' I said. 'What is it, a quest or a mission?'

'It's a quest *and* a mission.'

We went down the hill to look for a local map. The first gifty type shop we went into only had maps on postcards, but it was a start, so we bought one. Well, I did. Angie didn't have change.

'Garrett can pay me back for this,' I said.

'You should buy a little notebook,' she said. 'Then you could write down everything you spend on our Quest 'n' Mission and give him the bill when we get him back.'

Good idea, I thought, and bought a little notebook. Outside in the street I wrote 'Postcard' and 'Notebook' on the first page, and their prices. Then, underneath, I wrote, 'Ink from pen', but I didn't know what to charge for this so I decided to wait and see how often I used it on the Quest 'n' Mission to bring Pete back from non-existence.

'You know, Pete's got it made now,' I said.

'He has?'

'If he stays out of existence there'll be no more school, no more Face-Ache Dakin first thing in the morning, no more History with Hurley, no more kicking Mr Rice's balls, no more detentions.'

'Really good reasons for not existing,' Angie said.

'No more washing.'

'Pete doesn't do that so often anyway.'

'No more being told to cut his toenails, not pick his nose in public, keep the lousy jokes to himself. I bet he's glad of the break.'

We found a little wall to park our kazoos on and study the postcard. There wasn't much to study. It was a child's map of Wonkton-on-Sea, with pictures of the highlights, like the fountain in the central square, the railway station, the abattoir, stuff like that, all with these sweet little drawings that kids of four would like. There were some street names, but they were nothing out of the ordinary. Nothing devilish.

'I expected something to stand out,' Angie said.

'Something we could point at and say, "Wow, that's it".'

'It's not an actual map,' I reminded her.

'No. It isn't. Let's find one.'

Just past the Ogs Ead pub we found a

newsagent's that sold maps, including a map of Wonkton, though it was a bit pricey.

'You can buy this,' I said to Angie.

'You're the one with the notebook,' she replied.

'Well let's take a look at it first.'

We started to unfold the map. It was one of those complicated jobs you need a physics degree to open.

'Do you want that?' a voice said.

We looked up. The man at the counter was glaring at us with eyes like smashed conkers.

'We don't know till we look at it,' Angie replied.

'Then you might not want it at all,' he said.

'No, but at least we'll know then.'

'Then it'll be shop-soiled. I'll have to mark it down.'

'Mark it down?'

'Drop the price.'

'You can do that now if you like.'

'I won't have to if you don't open it.'

'They're opening and looking,' Angie said. 'You haven't told them not to.'

She meant the three men who'd taken down glossy mags from the top shelf and were turning them this way and that to look at the pictures from different angles.

'That's different,' the counter man said, but the three magazine-lookers suddenly realised we were talking about them and put them back in a hurry and left the shop with their eyes on the floor. They didn't hold the door open for one another.

'You just lost me three customers,' the man said.

'They might not have bought anything,' said Angie.

'But they might. Those magazines aren't cheap.'

'Nor is this map. What'll you take for it?'

'What's the price on it?' She told him. 'That's what I'll take for it.'

'Too much.' She put the map back. 'Come on, Jig.'

'Damn kids,' the man said as we left the shop.

Outside I said: 'We still don't have a map.'

'There'll be other maps.'

'And other shopkeepers who won't want us to open them.'

'We might not need to buy one anyway,' she said.

'I thought you said we had to.'

'Only because I didn't think of the library.'

She pointed across the street. We crossed it, to Wonkton Library. It wasn't open yet. We had an hour to kill, so we decided to stroll around for a bit. While we were strolling we passed Striker's Magic Joke Shop. The Combo Fun Box was still in the window.

'When we get him back I think we ought to buy that for him,' Angie said.

'You can. I'm not made of money.'

The moment I said this I realised I'd just used one of my mother's old chestnuts. I was speaking Golden Oldie.

'You're getting really tight-fisted, aren't you?' Angie said.

'No, I'm just stating a fact. I'm not made of money.'

I'd said it again. It was like a virus. I might as well apply for the pension book and flatpack Zimmer kit right away.

While we were waiting for the library to open we went to look at the sea. It wasn't there. There was nothing but beach, beach and more beach, all the way to the sky. Angie suggested that we walk a little way out, so we did. After a while the pebbles turned completely to sand and after another while the sand became soggy, so we took our shoes off and carried them. Soon our feet were sinking in even soggier sand, and going *ssshhhlump* when we pulled them out. I kind of liked being all the way out there in so much nothingness. Just us, the soggy sand, and the sky. The only people were way behind us, a man with a dog one way and a woman with a dog the other way. The dogs weren't on leads, which meant they could go wherever they wanted, as far as they wanted, while their owners screamed their names and the dogs ignored them. I hoped they wouldn't notice us because there was nowhere to hide if they came for us. We couldn't run because they'd catch us, and if we just stood there they would terrify us with all their barking and growling and their tongues hanging out, dripping saliva, sniffing our zips, and then they would knock us over and spend the next ten minutes dragging us round in the sand by our hair until their owners trotted up laughing and said, 'It's all right, he's just being friendly.'

'Nice out here,' Angie said.

'Cool,' I said.

'Cooler still if Pete was here.'

'I wasn't thinking of Pete.'

'I can't *stop* thinking about him,' she said.

'Don't tell him that, he'll never let you forget it.'

'If he was here I'd probably be thumping him and telling him to shut up, but he's not here, and I miss that.'

'Yeah, I miss the thumping.'

'And suppose we don't *get* him back. Suppose we don't find this trident of Neville's. Then what?'

'Then we're just the Two Musketeers.'

'The Two Musketeers isn't quite the same somehow.'

'We could get another musketeer.'

'No one could replace Pete,' Angie said.

'Get off. Anyone could replace Pete. Eejit Atkins could replace Pete. My garden gnome could replace Pete.'

We walked on. The sand was softer and softer all the time, wetter and wetter, and our feet sank deeper and deeper. When I said I thought it might be a good idea if we stopped Angie said, 'Just a bit further,' and on we went. There weren't many gulls about.

Hardly any gullish cackling, which made it pretty quiet apart from the *ssshhhlumping* of our feet in the soggy sand. In spite of all the walking we didn't seem to be getting any nearer the sea, but there were some white sails quite a way out which looked like they were sailing on sand. There was one striped sail, yellow and blue. I liked the look of that sail. Wouldn't have minded being out there under it with the wind in my shirt and lugholes. The dogs were a long way behind us now. If they came after us this far out their skinny legs would probably sink into the sand all the way up to their doggy chins and their owners wouldn't be able to pull them out, which'd be fine with me.

Chapter Fifteen

The library was open when we got back from the beach. We went in. We didn't ask where the maps were. Angie likes to find things for herself. She found a town map right away, in a book of town maps, and we sat down at one of the tables to look it over. It wasn't that different from the postcard, except that it wasn't as small, and it didn't have kiddiewink drawings showing the high spots, and a place for an address and a message on the back. It had a lot more streets too, but nothing hinted that it was where Neville was from.

'Maybe we should cast our net a bit wider,' Angie said.

'What net?'

'I mean he didn't say the place was actually *in* Wonkton, did he?'

We looked at another map. This one showed some of the places around Wonkton, villages like Piddle Quickly, Much Hooey, Church Scrotum, but none of them gave us the Big Hint until...

'That's it,' Angie said. 'That has to be where Neville's from.'

I gawped at the name. Oh yes, that was it all right.

'But how do we get there?' I said. 'We can't just hop on a bus or catch a train or walk there. This isn't an Enid Blyton story. The only places our parents let us go on our own are school and the shops, and it took years for them to let us go there without tagging along and making us look right and left and right again before we crossed roads.'

'We have two options,' Angie said.

'Many as that?'

'Option One, we persuade them to visit this place because it's the most fascinating dump for miles.'

'What's the point of them going?'

'They take us with them, berk.'

'I was kidding,' I said.

'Well don't. Pete's the comedian round here.'

'I see no Pete.'

'Yeah, well, here or not he doesn't need a bad-joke-double.'

'What's the other option?'

'Option Two, we tell the GOs we're going to spend the day wandering round town or the beach, like now, then go there on the sly by whatever transport's available.'

'What if it's only a horse and cart?'

'Then we go by horse and cart.'

We went back to the flat to see which of the plans we could put into action. The door from the street was lodged open, and there was a shoe in the door of the flat, so we didn't have to ring, knock or kick wood. We needed to talk to the mothers. The dads are the ones you turn to if you want stuff covered up, but the mothers are the ones you turn to if you want stuff done. The TV was already on.   The dads were sprawled in front of it, watching what looked like synchronised squirrel hurling. Those two'll watch anything if it seems sporty. Sporty is usually my signal to switch off.

'Where's Mum and Peg?' Angie asked. As usual, she was the only one of us with enough breath to speak.

'Uh?' said a dad, not taking his eyes off the squirrel action.

'Where are Mum and Peg?'

'Out.'

'Will they be back soon?'

'Uh?'

'Will…they…be…back…soon?'

'Dunno.'

'Option Two?' I said to Angie.

'Option Two.'

She wrote a note for our mothers saying we were just mooching round town and would be back for tea or sooner, and propped it up on the mantelpiece.

'See ya later!' we said to the dads.

They didn't hear. We went downstairs again, tiptoeing past the Professor's door as we'd tiptoed past it coming up, not because we didn't want to wake anybody but because we like tiptoeing.

Outside, Angie said: 'They can't have gone to the beach again. Not this early.'

'Who?'

'The Thong Creatures of Wonkton.'

'Don't let's go there and find out.'

'Deal.'

We went to the bus station instead. We knew where the bus station was because we'd passed it at least three times when walking round town. It wasn't a big bus station, but that was OK because the buses weren't very big either. Single deckers, and shorter than the ones at home. Yellow. Maybe we were in an Enid Blyton story after all. We had a bit of money, not much. The Golden Oldies called it 'holiday spending', but they're still in the last century. In this one you can't rent a DVD for that little. But the place we wanted was only three inches away on the map, so it couldn't cost much to get there – could it?

Every bus had the words *Curly's Buses* on the side, but none of them had the destination we wanted on the front. Angie went up to a driver – not Noddy or Big Ears – hauling himself into one of the yellow buses after flicking a dog-end at a cloud. She asked if he was going to the place we wanted. He said he wasn't. She asked which bus was going there. He said he didn't know. Then he climbed in and slid his door shut.

There were three more drivers sitting side by side on a bench, also smoking. Angie asked if any of them were going to our place. One of them said he was, with his bus, and he was leaving in fifteen minutes, but he gave us a funny look.

'Relatives there?'

'No,' said Ange.

'What you want to go there for then?'

'Just want to go there.'

'Wouldn't catch me getting off the bus there.' He glanced at his mates. They all grinned. 'No one in their right mind gets off there.'

'Why? What's wrong with it?'

'Let's just say they don't encourage visitors.'

We hung around till he got on his bus. Three others got on too. Passengers, not drivers. The tickets cost more than we expected. We realised why when we still hadn't arrived forty-five minutes later.

'It was only three inches,' I said to Angie.

The bus had picked up other people on the way, and every now and then one or two had got off. We were the only ones to get off at our stop. The driver told us that there was a bus back in an hour and twenty minutes if we'd seen all the sights by then, then he laughed and his doors closed and the bus pootled off. We looked around us.

So this was Devil's Bridge.

There only seemed to be one street and little grey houses stood along both sides of it. Almost all the houses had satellite dishes and most of the curtains were drawn. Nothing moved. There were no people about. There were no cars. Not even any parked cars. It looked like no one lived there. Like no one wanted to.

'Doesn't feel too welcoming,' I said.

'Well, we didn't come here to socialise,' said Angie. 'That must be the bridge.'

You couldn't miss it. It crouched there at the far end of the street, just beyond the last house. There was nothing on the other side of it, just dark empty fields. We walked towards it, along the street. The silence made me shiver.

'Ever feel you're being watched?' I asked.

'Quiet,' Angie said. 'They're probably listening too.'

It was a pretty ugly bridge. Grey and chunky, rearing up like some angry monster that had suddenly been turned to stone. There was a sharp twist at each end, where saggy old steps climbed up to the top.

'Most devilish bridge *I* ever saw,' Angie said.

'Yeah. Wonder where this trident is?'

It had to be there somewhere. Stuck on top like a flag? Taped underneath it? But we couldn't just poke around because there was someone up there, an old geezer, gazing over the side at all the floating packets and bottles and rubbish bobbing about in a bit of dirty stream.

'Maybe he's a devil,' I whispered.

'Doesn't look much of one,' Angie whispered back.

'Could be a retired one.'

He looked about as ordinary as anyone could look. Ordinary jacket, ordinary tie, ordinary grey hair sticking out the sides of an ordinary cloth cap. But Neville didn't look much like a devil either till you saw his horns.

'Morning!'

I whirled in shock. Angie had just called up to the man.

'What are you *doing*?' I hissed. 'Have you forgotten the words "Don't talk to strangers" chiselled into our pillow cases?'

'Well we can't just stand here waiting for him to go.'

'Yes, but when you shout "Morning!" to someone they usually shout "Morning!" back and then they start this very boring conversation and we can't get away.'

'I said good morning!'

Angie again. I raised my eyes to the clouds. The clouds understood.

The man didn't answer, like he hadn't answered the first time, but he raised a hand, which to me looked like 'Shove off', but Angie must have thought it meant 'Hey, good to see you, come up and have a good old natter about nothing interesting', because she bounced up the saggy steps to do just that. I followed. I did not bounce. More climbing.

'I suppose you want to know how the bridge came to be built,' the old geezer was saying as I made it to the top.

He said it with a heavy sigh, like he'd be happier talking about his heart condition. Up close his eyebrows looked like bits of unravelled Brillo pad, and he had a big red nose and a droopy grey moustache. He couldn't have been more ordinary if he tried.

'Not how it came to be built,' Angie said. 'How it got its name.'

'Same thing,' the man said.

'How do you mean?'

'Long story.'

'We'd love to hear it.'

I groaned. You have to be in the mood for long stories, and I wasn't.

'I'll begin at the beginning,' the man said.

'Must you?' I almost replied, but didn't.

'Way back in the mists of time,' he said, 'there was another bridge here, rickety old wooden thing, and a good river flowing beneath it. No village then, just one house up the lane there, where an old wife lived. The old wife's husband had died the previous year but she was still known as the old wife, because that's the way it was in those days.'

'Don't tell me,' I said. 'This is going to be an old wife's tale.'

The man squinted at me under his cap and Brillo brows.

'You know this story?'

'No.'

'Well do you want to hear it or don't you?'

'Yes, we do,' Angie said before I could blurt the truth. 'Please go on.'

'Well this particular old wife kept chickens,' the man said, to her more than me now that he knew I wasn't so keen, 'and she sold one chicken a week at the market in the next village, over the rickety wooden bridge. If she didn't sell a chicken a week she went hungry, see. But one night there was a humdinger of a storm, and lightning struck the bridge three times, and in the morning when the old wife came to cross with her chicken for the market in the next village she found nothing left of the bridge. Nothing standing.'

'So a devil appeared and built this one for her,' I said.

The man frowned at me again. 'You do know it.'

'No, but it's the way stories like this go.'

'Let the gentleman tell it,' Angie said.

'Just trying to move it along a bit,' I said.

'Well don't.'

'The old wife was upset that she was going to go hungry,' the man went on, 'and she set her chicken down on the ground in its basket and burst into tears. She was still in tears when she heard a very deep voice – '

'Devil,' I said quietly.

' – and the very deep voice said, "What you blubbin' 'bout, wummun?" (That's the way he spoke, see.) And the old wife dashed the tears from her eyes and saw a man standing in the waters up to his waist, except there never was a man that had horns and a long twitchy tail like that 'n.'

'And he built the bridge for the old wife in return for her soul,' I said, 'and that's how it came to be called Devil's Bridge. Right?'

'Not her soul,' said the man.

'What then?'

'Her chicken.'

'He built this bridge in return for a chicken?'

'Arr. That old devil, he loved chicken, he did. Chicken was his favourite dish, and where he came from there were no chickens. But it's against devilish law for a devil to take what he wants, or even ask for exactly what he wants, so he says to the old wife, he says, "I'll build you a fine bridge to cross this river, and it'll stand for years and years, and all I ask in payment is the first living creature that comes across it when it's done." "And when will it be done?" the old wife asked.

"Come back in an hour," the devil said. "Can't I watch?" said the old wife. "If you watch me work," the devil said, "the bridge'll not be done and no other bridge will ever rise here again, and you'll starve to death. Go away and come back in an hour with your chicken and you'll find a bridge to cross." '

'I bet she watched in secret,' Angie said.

'She did not,' said the man. 'That old wife knew that a devil's word is his bond, and she went away and she didn't look until she returned an hour later along with her chicken.'

'And the bridge was finished and she gave the devil her chicken,' I said wearily.

'No,' said the man.

'No?'

'No. The bridge was finished all right, and the old wife knew that the devil had his eye on her chicken, and she intended to let him have it in thanks and go hungry that week. The devil expected it too, and he stood on top of the new bridge – this bridge – smiling his dark smile and lashing his long tail and polishing his sharp horns, eager as eager for a taste of that succulent chicken.

But when the old wife put the chicken on the bridge for it to walk up to the devil something happened that neither he nor the old wife had anticipated.'

The boring old storyteller paused, obviously waiting for one of us to ask what the something was. I might have got in first but by this time all that wanted to come out my mouth was yawns. If I'd had a staple gun I would have used it on my lips. So it was up to Angie.

'What happened?'

'A rat jumped up from the dark waters below the bridge,' the man replied, 'and leapt at the chicken, meaning to have it for himself. But the chicken saw the rat a'coming, and squawked over the side of the bridge in a fowl panic, and the rat, which was running fast, just missed her and carried on up the bridge – right into the devil's arms.'

He paused again. 'Then what?' Angie said.

'Then the devil was obliged to take the rat in payment and off he went to pop it in a stew,' the man said. 'He wasn't happy about that because he wasn't too partial to rat stew, even with onions and parsnips and half a cup of herbs, but the deal was done and the bridge was built and he'd taken the first living creature that came over it, and there was nothing he could do about it.'

'And the bridge has been here ever since,' Angie said.

'The bridge has, though the river dried up years ago.'

'Terrific story,' I said. It was over. Suddenly I didn't need to yawn any more. I can't have sounded like I meant it, though, because the man glared at me round his big red nose.

'Stories like that had boys of my generation agog,' he said. 'Not nowadays. Stories don't count any more unless they're on a screen or famous and there's explosions and car chases and all. Shame.'

'I thought it was a good story,' Angie said.

The man's eyes flicked from me to her. 'You did?'

'Yes. Great.'

'It was garbage,' he said.

'What?'

'Complete cobblers, start to finish, and that's the very last time I'm telling it.'

He pushed angrily between us and limped down the steps. At the bottom he rushed to the nearest gloomy little house and knocked the door back with his stick. As he went in I was sure I heard him say, 'Bloody tourists,' but I might have imagined that. I didn't imagine him slamming the door, though. Or bolting it.

Chapter Sixteen

We learnt the real story of the bridge when we went back down the steps ourselves. We'd missed it on the way up, but at the bottom there was a notice under transparent plastic on this stone column. This is it.

NOTICE TO VISITORS

Until 1911 the name of this village was Peesdyke. The people of Peesdyke were very poor and they changed the name to Devil's Bridge and made up a story about the bridge to attract foolish tourists and their money. It worked too. But that was then. We don't want tourists any more. We want to be left alone with the Internet, eBay and Sky. So listen. This is just an old bridge. It wasn't built in an hour by a devil. It took months to build, and it was built by men. Ordinary men, without tails and horns. Got it? So why don't you go back where you came from and leave us in peace? Eh? Go on. Scat.

'Feel like taking a hint?' Angie said to me.

'Already taken.'

But we couldn't just leave. We needed wheels. Bus wheels. Which meant waiting. Wait, in that place? Where you had the feeling you were being watched from all those gloomy windows by creepy people who didn't want you there? Let me tell you, while an hour is a pretty short time to build a bridge, it's a heck of a time to wait for a bus in a place like Devil's Bridge (or Peesdyke) where there's nothing, but nothing, to do or even look at. There wasn't even anywhere to sit, like a bench, which meant I had to flop on the kerb beside the road. Angie walked up and down, up and down. No kerbs for her. Not these days.

'You're turning into a Golden Oldie,' I said as she walked by one time.

'Eh?'

'Wasn't so long since you didn't care where you sat.'

'I was little then.'

'Not so little.'

She was still walking up and down, up and down, and I was still sitting there, sitting there, when a wind sprang up. I like that. 'A wind sprang up.' I didn't invent it, don't know who did, but I like it. 'A wind sprang up.' But there was dust on the springing wind, and some of the dust got in my eyes. Funny, that. Well not so funny, not for me. Whenever dust decides to fly about it always flies into my eyes, no one else's. I can be standing around or walking along with sixteen other people and this wind springs up and this dust flies and the dust always goes straight in my eyes, just mine, like my eyes are dust-magnets or something. I rubbed my eyes, and I rubbed them some more, and I could hear my mother's voice – 'Don't rub them, Jiggy, you'll only make it worse' – but I went on rubbing and rubbing because when you have dust in your eyes it feels better than letting them just sit there, all dusty, trying to see.

'What's up?' Angie said, walking by.

'Dust in my eyes.'

'Well don't rub them, you'll only make it worse.'

When the wind died (I like that too: 'the wind died') and the dust stopped flying, and I began to get my sight back, I saw something through the tears. Something in my shoe, my trainer, the left one, a small card, sticking up in the side. The wind had blown it there. I took the card out and would have flicked it away if not for Angie.

'Don't you dare,' she said. 'I hate litter bugs.'

'It's not my litter,' I said.

'You've got it, you're about to chuck it, so it's yours.'

'There aren't any bins.'

'So put it in your pocket and deposit it later, when you find one.'

'Hark at you,' I said. '"Deposit it later".'

'Yes, hark at me and do as I say.'

I grumbled, of course, but I did as she said. I wasn't going to drop just any old rubbish in my pocket, though. It could have been anything. Could have had anything on it. But all it *had* on it was words.

Striker's Magic Joke Shop

FISHEYE STREET ⚡ WONKTON-ON-SEA.

Everything you never knew
you wanted in Jokes 'n' Magic.
Hours vary.

'Look at this,' I said.

Angie glanced at the card. 'That shop,' she said.

'Bit weird, isn't it?'

'What's weird about it?'

'Us being all the way out here in the middle of nothing and this card – from the one shop in Wonkton Pete was interested in – blowing into my trainer when it could have blown absolutely anywhere.'

'What are you saying?'

'I'm saying what if it's a message from Pete.'

'How can it be a message from Pete? Pete's been removed from existence.'

'Well maybe he's found a way to send us this, as a sign. You know, like ghosts at séances tapping tables. It has to be from Pete. Too much of a coincidence for it just to turn up here, three long inches from town.'

'Bus's coming.'

I stuffed the card in my pocket and stood up for the bus. When it stopped we got on. Seemed silly not to after waiting for it all that time. It was the same bus we'd come on. Same driver.

'Was it worth it?' he asked with a smirky grin.

'Just like JoyWorld,' I said, without one.

He laughed merrily and the doors hissed shut.

One thing we'd forgotten to bring with us was food, so we were pretty close to starving when we finally got back to Wonkton. Because of this we went straight to the flat, where the grub was free. This time it was the mums who were in and the dads who were out. The dads had said they were 'going to see the sights', which meant the sights of a bar Mum said. They didn't ask where we'd been, just if we'd had a good time. I said, 'Not so great,' and Mum looked sadly at Audrey and Audrey looked sadly at her. The reason they'd gone out earlier was to get two extra keys made for the street door and two extras for the flat door. One pair was for the dads and one pair for Angie and me, which meant we all had to go everywhere in twos if we didn't want to be locked out.

'What are your plans for the rest of the day?' Audrey asked while we rammed food down our throats.

'No plans,' Angie said, spitting bread over her. 'Why?'

'We thought we might play clock golf down by the beach.'

'Go ahead,' we said together.

'Don't you want to play?' Mum said.

'No.' This was me.

'But you're on holiday.'

'Doesn't mean we have to play clock golf,' Angie said.

'What do you want to do then?' Audrey asked.

'Don't worry about us,' I said. 'We'll sort ourselves out.'

We waited for them to go out. They didn't take beach towels, which was good news. Meant they wouldn't be tossed into jail for indecent exposure. Also meant the beach wasn't off-limits to us.

'We'd better go see Neville,' Angie said. 'Try for some info about where to look for this trident of his.'

'He won't tell us. He said so.'

'Maybe we can twist his arm.'

'Might come off in our hands.'

'He has to give us something to go on, Jig. We've looked at the maps, we got it wrong about Devil's Bridge, haven't a clue what to do next.'

All true. We left the flat. Angie took charge of

our keys because she said I'd lose them. 'Doesn't feel right without Pete,' she said on the way to the beach.

'I could get used to it,' I said.

'Oh, come on, you have to admit it's not the same without him.'

'Yes, I admit that.'

'What if we don't get him back?' she said.

'Then it's bye-bye PG.'

'That's a horrible thing to say.'

'It's not horrible, it's the truth.'

'But Pete's our bud. I know he has his faults, but...one for all and all for lunch?'

I sighed. 'Did you have to say that?'

'Obviously I did,' she said.

One for all and all for lunch. Our Musketeery motto. Means we have to look out for one another. Hang together through thick and thicker. Because Angie had reminded me of it I suddenly felt bad for not missing Pete much. The three of us have known one another all our lives. We've done everything together except take baths and go to the toilet. If it had been me that had been removed from existence it would have been Pete, not me, who'd be having

211

this conversation with Angie. The only difference would be that there'd be more stupid jokes and she'd be slapping him round the back of the head every three steps.

Professor Shanks had already set up his booth for the day and he was doing stuff round the back of it, getting ready for the show probably. A few kids were already sitting on the sand and pebbles waiting for it to start.

'Come to take me up on my offer of a free show for helping me out yesterday?' the Prof asked as we ambled up.

'That's it,' I said.

'Help you pack up afterwards if you like,' said Angie.

'I'd appreciate that. Getting too much for me, all this.'

'Still thinking of closing down?'

'Very much so. I should have more of a life than this. It came to me last night that I don't enjoy much any more. It was Travolta Night at the Hog's Head. You should have seen me. Seen the whole thing. Fifty dazzling white suits strutting their stuff under revolving lights. Unfortunately I had to leave early, so I missed the single-file finale.'

'Why did you have to leave early?' I asked.

'The bouncers said I was getting over-excited. I was only *dancing*, for God's sake.'

While he was telling us this he was holding one of the flaps at the back of the booth open and I got a glimpse inside. Neville was sitting on a little shelf below the curtained stage. He raised a hand and waved. If it had been any other living puppet it might have been a friendly wave, but a wave from him sent shivers down my spine. Still, we had to talk to him, and we had to be alone to do that.

'Got everything from the van?' Angie asked the Prof.

'Almost. Just a couple more things. Watch this for me?'

We said we would. Before he went he looked in the booth. He whispered something we couldn't catch, then headed up to the road. Angie and I stuck our heads between the flaps. The light was all red inside because the sun was leaking through the stripes of the tent material. All the puppets seemed to be there, including Judy, who didn't look like she had any more life than the rest of them.

'Has he gone?' Neville said.

We told him that he had but he wouldn't be long. I asked what the Prof had said to him.

'He told me to keep quiet and still because you were here. Did you find it? The place?'

'Well, we went to Devil's Bridge...'

'Devil's Bridge? What did you go there for?'

'It seemed the logical place,' Angie said.

Neville growled. 'Devil's Bridge! I should have seen that coming. So obvious! You're looking for something to do with me, your eyes light on the word "Devil", and off you go. Listen. I've never been to Devil's Bridge. From what I hear no one in their right mind would go to Devil's Bridge. Devil's Bridge is not the place!'

'Isn't he a bully?' said another voice. Judy's.

'Put a sock in it, crone,' Neville snapped.

Judy pulled herself upright.

'If I was bigger I wouldn't take his nonsense,' she said. 'I'd put him over my knee and tan his little behind good and proper, that I would!'

'Well here is the news,' said Neville. 'You're not bigger. A ladybird would crush that wrinkly old knee. So close the raggedy lips. Swallow the puppety teeth. Shut the ancient cake-hole.'

'There isn't time for this,' Angie said to him. 'We only came here today for one thing. We need more info. You have to give us a clue about this place of yours. Where it is, what it is.'

'I already gave you a clue,' he said.

'You did? What clue?'

'I can't tell you that.'

'When did you give it to us?'

'All I can say is I sent it to you.'

'You sent it to us?' I said. 'When? How?'

Neville pulled an invisible zip across his little mouth.

'Look, do you want your size back or not?' Angie said.

He hesitated. Then he said: 'OK. It's risky, but...'

He took a breath. 'Think about how small I am.'

'How small you are?'

'I mean how would you describe someone my size?'

'I don't know,' said Angie. 'Little?'

'Try harder.'

'Titch?' I said.

'Harder.'

We tried harder. Both of us. It went something like this.

'Half-pint?'

'No.'

'Short-stuff?'

'No.'

'Tiddles?'

'I'm not a cat.'

'Sawn-off?'

'No.'

'Pee-wee?'

'No.'

'Tinky-winky?'

'Now you're being insulting.'

'Pocket-size?'

'Ah.'

'What do you mean, "Ah"?'

'That's all I'm saying.'

'All you're saying is "Ah"?'

'It's all I *can* say. You're on your own now.'

'Quiet, he's back.'

'Hello, there.' (The Professor's voice, behind us.)

Judy fell back into lifeless puppet mode. Even Neville's face lost all expression so the Prof wouldn't know he'd been chatting to us. We backed out into the sunshine.

'Just having a look at them, hope you don't mind,' Angie said.

'No, that's all right. Now I must get started or the council will be ticking me off for not sticking to my timetable. The seaside's like a police state these days. Go round the front. Watch the show.'

We went round the front and watched the show. Punch and Judy it wasn't. No one hit anybody. No one really argued. The policeman was nice and jolly, whistling a lot. The baby had sweet dreams and never got tipped out of its pram. Ms Sweet (Judy) didn't argue with Mr Nicey-Nicey (Neville) and Mr Nicey-Nicey was as sugary as treacle tart to her. Neville still dressed the same for the part of Mr Nicey-Nicey, but he didn't show his horns and he didn't look mean. He kept laughing and saying how lovely Ms Sweet looked, and she kept saying how kind and generous he was. There wasn't much of a story.

My guess was that the Prof hadn't had the heart to write one, so the show wasn't very interesting.

Sitting cross-legged on the sand and pebbles

with all the little kids it was hard not to topple over head first in a snooze. Neville only looked our way once, and for a second his eyes were very black, like they were trying to tell us something. Or remind us of something he'd said.

Chapter Seventeen

After the show we helped the Professor stow his stuff again, then took off on our own. While we tried and failed to work out what Neville meant about his size being a clue we drifted along the beach and round the town until...

'Hello, you two! Changed your minds?'

...we came to the clock golf course.

Angie glanced at me. 'Think of anything better to do?'

'Not really.'

So we played clock golf with the mothers. We let them win.

That evening Mum and Audrey spent a lot of time washing their hair, curling it, blow-drying it, straightening it, doing it again, asking one another's advice, and trying on clothes. Nobody asked them what it was all for, but when they finally appeared, we stopped what we were doing, saying and thinking, and just gaped. They stood arm in arm, faces so thick with make-up they looked like death masks, big shiny lips, hair like helium balloons, in dresses two sizes too small, and lots of jangly jewellery.

'Are we…going somewhere?' Dad asked nervously.

'Don't know about you,' Mum answered, 'but we are.'

'You're going out without us?' Oliver said.

'Definitely without you,' said Aud.

'Whew,' said Dad.

'Where?' Oliver asked.

'On the town,' said Mum.

'On *this* town?' said Dad.

'To a club,' said Audrey.

'What club?' said Oliver suspiciously.

'It's a pub really,' Mum said, 'but they have these theme nights. Last night they had a Seventies night. Dancing.'

'Are you talking about the Ogs Ead?' Angie asked.

Audrey frowned at her. 'The Hog's Head,' she said, shaping the aitches with her big shiny lips.

'What's tonight's event that's such a big girlie deal?' Dad said.

'That's it,' said Mum. 'It's All-Girls' Night.'

Dad and Oliver swapped chuckles.

'Well, I don't mind giving *that* a miss, do you?'

'I think I'll get by without it.'

But they still wanted to know what went on at an All-Girls' Night.

'Tonight it's the Sheratons,' Audrey said, winking at Mum.

'The what?'

'The Sheratons. You've heard of the Sheratons.'

'Have we?'

'The male stripper group,' I said.

My dad's thumb jerked. It was the one hovering over the On-Off switch on the remote. The TV died.

'Male strippers?'

'Yes,' said Mum.

'You're going to an event that has male strippers?'

'Yes.'

'I don't like the sound of that,' said Oliver.

'We do,' said Audrey. 'See you later. If you're lucky.'

And off they went. We heard their heels clickety-clicking down the stairs like clothes pegs going on strike.

For a minute there was a hush in the flat while at

least three brains tried to blot out the image of male strippers. Then my father said: 'So what do we do? I don't want to sit here all night.'

'You've sat here all day,' I pointed out.

'That's because the sun was out. Any thoughts?' he asked Oliver.

'Well, we've only tried one pub so far,' said Oliver. 'Could spread our wings a bit.'

'I'd give the Ogs Ead a miss if I were you,' I said.

'What about you two?' Dad said. 'Will you be all right here by yourselves if we go out?'

'We'll get by.'

Unlike the mothers, the dads didn't spend half the night in the bathroom or wash their hair or blow-dry it or ask for opinions or try on different clothes or cover themselves with jewellery. They just hoofed it.

'And we do…what?' Angie said when we were alone.

I shrugged. 'Watch telly?'

'How can we watch telly when Pete's still missing?'

I reached for the remote. 'Might be something good on.'

'Turn that on,' Angie said, 'and I'll never speak to you again.'

I turned it on. She scowled.

'Jig, don't you *care* about Pete?'

'Hey, *Terminator 4*. I'd forgotten this was on.'

'I don't believe you,' she said.

'No, it is, really. I saw the trailer at home last week. We'd have missed it if we'd gone to JoyWorld.'

'I mean I don't believe that you don't care that Pete's... *Terminator 4*?'

'Yeah. Best one of the trilogy, according to Eejit Atkins.'

Angie sank into a chair, eyeing the screen. So did I, same screen, different chair.

'He's too old for this stuff,' she said.

'Atkins?'

'Him. The Muscles from Brussels.'

'He's not the Muscles from Brussels. That's one of the others. Jean-Claude Van Sodde, Pete calls him.'

'The neck's a real giveaway. Might pump the rest up but the neck still goes goosey.'

'What do you say we listen to what they are saying?'

223

We listened. We also watched.

'He ought to keep the shirt on,' Angie said after a while.

'He can't. Shirt's got to come off at least three times every film, or be turned to rags, it's part of the deal.'

'But he's a Golden Oldie. Probably has grandkids. Oh, not the underpants.' She splayed her fingers over her eyes. 'No! No! Keep 'em on, keep 'em on!'

'Wonder what's happening at the Ogs Ead right now?' I mused.

'I don't even want to think about it,' Ange mused back.

I didn't either, so we tried not to.

Terminator 4 wasn't as good as Eejit said it was, but why would it be? Atkins is not someone I often turn to for film reviews, or any other opinion come to that. But it took our minds off things. Off Pete. OK, I admit it, I was worried about Pete. But there's worry and worry. I wasn't going to sit around with my chin in my hands thinking 'O Pete, where art thou?' Besides, if he was taking a break from existence he probably didn't know much about it.

Probably wasn't uncomfortable or anything. Bet he wasn't missing us. I bet he wasn't even missing chocolate!

After the film we couldn't think of anything else to do, so we left the telly on. Flipping through the channels we learnt how to plumb a water feature into a Chinese-style patio, hang rollerblinds, build kitchen cupboards, bleach our hair, chat one another up, ride a horse, breed spiders, lose weight and have bits of ourselves enlarged while bidding for antiques in designer jumpsuits. It was quite an educational evening. Two things we didn't learn were where to find Neville's trident and how to get Pete back. We'd gone round in a lot of circles that day and come nowhere near any answers.

Failing to work stuff out is pretty tiring, so we went to bed early. I was doing a fair job of getting a peaceful night's kip until my father threw my door back. When the door hit the wall my eyelids jerked up. So did the rest of me. My head hit the springs of the top bunk.

'Your mother isn't back yet!'

'Urrrggh?'

'It's gone midnight!'

'Urr.'

I flopped down again and he slammed the door.

But that wasn't the only time I was woken up. Next time I thought I was dreaming that something was pulling at my shoulder. I shook the dreamy something off. There was a little thud and a yelp, followed by a pause. Then something was pulling at my duvet. I yanked it back — hard. This time there wasn't a little thud and a yelp followed by a pause. The pause followed a yelp and a little thud instead.

But then I felt something walking on me. It was kind of like Stallone if I leave my bedroom door open. If Stallone's awake he likes to make sure he's not the only one. But this wasn't a cat. It wasn't anything with four legs. It was something with a voice. Only a small voice, but a loud enough one when it shouted, 'WAKE UP!' in my slumbering lug. The McCue eyelids jerked up again. It was quite dark with the door and curtains closed, but there was enough light to see Neville glaring at me three centimetres from my face.

'I'm guessing this isn't a dream,' I muttered.

'You're guessing right. Worked it out yet?'

'Worked what out?'

'Where to find my trident.'

'Oh, leave me alone!'

'You're useless, you know that?'

That did it. I sat up so sharply he fell backwards. He would have landed on the carpet if I hadn't grabbed one of his little legs as he went over the side. I yanked him back. He stood on my bunk, holding on to his hat and smoothing down his waistcoat.

'It'd almost be worth not getting Pete back to put a stop to you,' I said.

'Almost be worth it?'

He was right and he knew it. Angie and I had to do what we could for Pete, even if it meant turning a full-sized mischief-maker like Neville the Devil loose on the world.

'And no,' I said, 'we still don't know where to look for this perishing trident of yours.'

He bunched his little fists. 'You two are about as bright as a pair of no-watt light bulbs.'

'Some input from you might brighten us up a bit.'

'I've given you input,' he said. 'I sent you a clue.

Not just a clue either. An address.'

'An address?'

'An address you're obviously too dumb to recognise. I've known smarter glove puppets!'

'Tell us more then.'

'If I tell you any more,' Neville said, 'he'll know, and I'm one ex-devil. Nothing gets by him.'

'Who are you talking about?'

'My worst enemy. The one who holds the trident. If I steer you towards him, he'll turn me to dust with a flick of his fingers.'

'Sounds like someone we ought to know.'

'Believe me, you don't want to know him. You think I'm a devil? You ain't seen nothing till you meet him. You have to get to him – without any more help from me – and get the trident off him. You're on your own, kiddo.'

'I wish I was. Then I might get some sleep.'

'This is not the time to sleep,' he said.

'Yes, it is. It's called Night.'

'Yeah, well I'm getting impatient. Starting to lose my cool. You'd like me even less if I lost my cool.'

'This is you being cool, is it? The height of

a ruler, working as Mr Punch's understudy, living in a shoe-box?'

'It's not a shoe-box. It belonged to the Hangman before the Prof gave him his marching orders.'

'Did the Hangman go on a course too? Hangmen Anonymous? Push off, leave me in peace.'

'All right, I'll go. But here's a warning for you, Piggy.'

'Jiggy.'

'If you don't get me my size back by Wednesday lunchtime I'm turning your friend into a bed-mite and putting him in there with you.'

He gripped the duvet, dropped on to his front, and slid hand over hand to the floor.

'How did you get in anyway?' I asked him over the side. 'Those stairs are pretty steep for legs that small, and anyway the flat door's closed. So's my door.'

'Little trick I keep up my sleeve,' he said. 'Well, not my sleeve so much.'

'What is it?'

'This.'

He turned his back to me and dropped his pants. Then he waggled his little bottom and a long thin tail with an arrow-shaped head broke out and uncoiled like a snake. I was still staring at this when there was a little pop. The tail was gone. So was its owner.

Chapter Eighteen

I don't know what time Audrey and my mother got in, but they were still up before me and the dads next morning. Looked a bit different now though. The big hair was big flat hair, the eyes weren't all bright and sparkly, the shiny lips were like overcooked oven chips, and they weren't full of the joys.

'Have a good time?' I said to Mum.

'Don't talk to me,' she snapped.

But this passed. When our mothers are on holiday they make sure to keep the smiles in place because they think smiling is what people do on holiday. When we were all up and dressed they produced a glossy brochure they'd picked up yesterday.

'We thought we might go here today,' they said.

Oliver, who was nearest, took the brochure. He looked at it. Didn't seem impressed. 'First theme nights, now theme parks?' he said.

'JoyWorld's a theme park,' Audrey reminded him.

'JoyWorld has theme pubs.'

He passed the brochure to Dad, who read the name of the park.

'The Wizard World of Harry...?' He couldn't finish. 'Tell me you're kidding,' he said to Mum and Aud.

Mum took the brochure and started to read all about it. Aloud.

'"The streets, shops and rides of The Wizard World will delight kids of all ages! The park is one great big show – and we do mean *great*! – and every employee, from the character stars to the street cleaners to the staff of the Three Cauldrons Tavern wear appropriate costumes and have things to tell you about the –"'

'Tavern?' said Oliver.

Mum dried up and let us look at the brochure for ourselves. Pages turned. Jaws dropped. Looks of horror spread.

'When you say you thought "we" might go there,' Oliver said, 'this is another trip for the two of you – right?'

'We mean all six of us,' Audrey said.

'It's only ten miles away,' said Mum. 'Near an

ancient village called Relative Normalcy where witches were burnt at the stake. Nice family outing, we thought.'

The brochure was stuffed with pictures of old bearded geezers in long nighties handing out really wise advice to anyone who could be bribed to listen. There were castles and dragons and owls and evil creatures and thin enemies, and there were magic wands all over the place, and kids zipping happily about on broomsticks. There were a lot of pointy hats. The pictures were bad enough, but there were also these announcements on every page…

'Free Quill Pen with every ticket!'

'Sorting Ceremony – Talking Hats and Badges at low-low prices!'

'See Witches and Wizards and Warlocks perform tricks, cast spells and create illusions in Gullible Square!'

'Streets full of Magic! Shops full of tat!'*

'Visit the famous Wizard School!'

'A Genuine Wizard Classroom, Genuinely Wizard Lessons!'

'Broomstick Slopes for Tinies! (100% safe)'

---

* It actually said 'Mementoes'. I'm reading between the lines here.

'Grand Parade of Wizard Creatures!'

'This is my idea of hell!' This was Dad.

'I should have expected that, coming from you,' said Mum.

'You've got it from me too,' said Oliver.

'Think of the children,' said Audrey.

'If you mean us, don't bother,' said I.

'Wouldn't you like to see all these things?' Mum again.

'Seen 'em,' I said. 'On film. I don't want to make a career of it.'

'Angie, wouldn't you like to go?'

'There's something I'd rather do more,' said Ange.

'What's that?'

'Be chained by my ankles to the back of a tractor and dragged slowly over burning coals.'

'That's a "not keen" then, is it?'

'That's a "not keen".'

'I thought the idea of going on holiday together was that we'd do things together,' Audrey said.

'Where'd you get that from?' said Oliver.

Audrey looked at Mum and Mum looked at Audrey and they both looked sad that none of us were entering into the holiday spirit.

'We could go,' Audrey said.

'On our own?' said Mum.

'Well, why not?'

Mum thought this over, and as she thought it over her eyes brightened and the saggy shoulders went up like they'd suddenly grown a coat hanger. 'Yes,' she said. 'Why not?'

Just before they trotted down the stairs and headed for the Wizard World, Angie said something useful to them. 'If we're not going with you,' she said, 'what about giving us an extra wedge to spend here?'

If I say this kind of thing I get nothing. Well, nothing but laughed at. But nobody laughs at Angie, even her mum, because Ange has this way about her which people take seriously. I've tried it like she does it, but it doesn't work. Even when I do it in a mirror the person I'm talking to laughs at me. Anyway, the mothers coughed up and suddenly we were quite a bit richer than we'd been since the last time we went on holiday together and Angie asked that question.

Audrey had forgotten to take her camera, so Angie put it in her own pocket as we were leaving. I asked what there was to take pictures of in Wonkton.

'We're on holiday,' she said. 'What's a holiday without photos?'

'Best forgotten when it's one like this,' I replied.

It wasn't so bright out today because the sun was behind a big dark cloud. But that was OK. We weren't planning on sunbathing. Weren't planning anything. Didn't know what to do next about Pete either.

We were at the bottom of the hill wondering if our legs would ever stop when Angie said: 'You know that place our mums are going to?'

I said that I did.

'And you know we're trying to find the place Neville's from?'

'Yes. So?' I stopped walking. 'You don't think…?'

She stopped too, which saved her answering over her shoulder halfway along the street.

'Wizards, magic, spells. Very Neville, wouldn't you say?'

'You think Neville comes from a theme park?

'I don't know, but I can't imagine him coming from a bungalow with a neat little garden in

Wonkton-on-Sea, can you? And what about the old hippy at the airport?'

'What about him?'

'He might not have been a hippy. Might have been a stray wizard from the Wizard World. Jig, that could be why he was helping Neville. They come from the same place!'

'Hmm,' I said thoughtfully. It was a thoughtful moment. When it was over I whistled with relief and said, 'Maybe we should've gone with them.'

'Maybe we should've.'

'But if it's not the place, think what we'd have had to put up with all day.'

'If it is, we could find the trident, which means Neville would give Pete back to us.'

'We've missed our chance anyway,' I said. 'They've gone.'

'We could go on our own.'

'On our own? They'd have a fit.'

'They wouldn't know if we didn't tell them.'

'They'd see us there.'

'Might not. From the map in the brochure it looked pretty big.'

'I'd be looking over my shoulder the whole time

just in case. And if we did bump into them they'd think we'd changed our minds because we wanted to be with them, then they'd go everywhere with us out of gratitude and we'd never find the trident. Let's go tomorrow.'

'That'd mean another day with Pete out of existence,' Angie said.

'Another day you don't have to tell him to shut up,' I said.

'Well, there is something we could do today.'

'Whassat?'

'See Nev. Mention the theme park and check his reaction. He's not so good at hiding things. He might not be able to say it's the place, but he could give it away by his expression or the way he answers.'

'Worth a try. Think he's at the beach with the Prof and Judy yet?'

'One way to find out.'

On the way to the beach I told her about Neville's latest middle-of-the-night visit and the terrible person he was afraid of but couldn't name. Angie asked if he'd dropped any extra hints. I said that if he had I'd missed them. 'But he did say he'd given us the address of the place the trident's at,' I said.

'Address? What address? When did he give it to us?'

'I don't know what and I don't know when.'

'Oh, brilliant.'

There was no sign of the Mr Nicey-Nicey and Ms Sweet booth on the beach. It was either too early or the Prof had heard a weather report. The sky was getting darker by the minute. We leant on the sea wall, looking out at...yes, you guessed it.*

'What do we do now?' I said.

'Why don't we toss for it?' said Angie.

'Toss for it?'

'Flip a coin for what to do next.'

'To flip a coin for what to do next we need some choices.'

'So pick a couple of things.'

I tried. Couldn't think of anything I wanted to do in Wonkton-on-Sea. Anything at all.

'You pick a couple of things.'

She tried. Couldn't think of anything either.

'Flip one anyway,' she said. 'If it comes up tails the first person to see something with a tail gets to keep it. The coin, I mean. If it comes up heads...'

'I have a teensy problem with that,' I said.

---

* The sea, if you didn't.

'What problem?'

'If I flip a coin of mine and I win I haven't won anything.'

'Life isn't all about winning, Jig.'

'It's not all about losing either. And another thing. Seagulls have tails. Sort of. The dogs on the beach and the million and one on leads pulling their owners round town have tails. And that's just tails. Everything that lives and breathes has a head, including us.'

'We could exclude people, animals and birds.'

'And fish,' I said.

'And fish.'

'And insects.'

'And insects.'

'But if we exclude all those what else is there?'

'There's a boil,' she said.

'A boil?'

'A boil on your skin.'

'I haven't got a boil on my skin.'

'No, I mean a boil on *someone's* skin.'

'Whose?'

'Anyone's, doesn't matter. Boils have heads is what I'm saying. So do spots. The really ripe ones. They

240

grow and grow and develop a head, and the head sometimes bursts.'

'All over mirrors if you squeeze them,' I said.

'And flowers,' said Ange.

'I've never squeezed a spot over a flower.'

'Flowers have heads. The froth on beer is called a head too.'

'Anything else?'

'There could be. Be fun finding something else.'

'That's your idea of fun, is it?'

'No,' she said. 'It's my idea of desperation.'

I didn't get a coin out and flip it. I shoved my hands in my jacket pockets to give them (the hands) something to do. My jacket pockets are usually empty, apart from a snot-rag when I have a cold, and a scrap of paper or an elastic band sometimes. Or an old bus ticket. Or a sweet wrapper. They were empty today except for one thing.

'I'd forgotten this,' I said when I pulled it out.

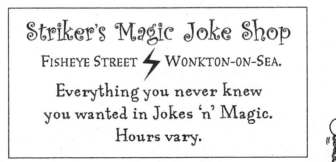

Striker's Magic Joke Shop

FISHEYE STREET ⚡ WONKTON-ON-SEA.

Everything you never knew
you wanted in Jokes 'n' Magic.
Hours vary.

Angie chuckled. 'Your message from Pete.'

'Ange...'

'What?'

'I have a thought.'

'Sit down, you'll get dizzy.'

'Suppose Pete was trying to tell us that this shop had something to do with his disappearance.'

'Striker's Joke Shop?'

'*Magic* Joke Shop. Magic, Ange, *magic*.'

'It might not have come from Pete,' she said.

'Yeah, I know. You said.'

'No, I mean it might have come from Neville.'

'Neville?'

'Remember he said he'd sent us a clue about where to find the trident? Suppose the clue was this card? And what about that guessing game of his?'

'What guessing game?'

'The one where he wanted us to describe his size. The only one he thought much of was 'pocket-sized' – remember?'

'Ye-es...'

'And where did you put the card?'

'In my pocket.'

'In your pocket. Where you just took it from. And what's on the card? An address.'

It didn't take long for this to sink in. When it was well and truly sunk, I nodded. If I'm such a genius why hadn't I thought of all that? We turned from the beach.

Headed for Striker's Magic Joke Shop...

Chapter Nineteen

...which was closed. In the glass door of the shop, on the inside, there was a notice.

> ### OPENING TIMES
> SOME DAYS AROUND 9 OR 10,
> OCCASIONALLY AS EARLY AS 7,
> BUT SOME DAYS AS LATE AS 12.
>
> ### CLOSING TIMES
> WE USUALLY CLOSE ABOUT 5 or 6,
> BUT SOMETIMES AS LATE AS 11 OR 12.
>
> ### OTHER TIMES
> WE AREN'T HERE AT ALL.
> HERE'S A TIP.
> IF YOU SEE THIS NOTICE COME BACK
> WHEN WE ARE HERE.

'Well, the card does say "hours vary",' Angie said.

'But when do we come back?'

'When they're here, like it says. Whenever that is.' We stood looking at the window display, including The Combo Fun Box Pete had wanted. 'I think we should buy that for him when we get him back.'

'If we get him back.'

'*When* we get him back.'

'What, buy it as a gift, you mean?'

'Yeah. Welcome home present.'

'At that price?'

'We could go halves.'

'At *that* price?'

'You wouldn't chip in to buy your lifelong friend a welcome home present?' Angie said.

'Chipping in isn't the same as going halves. Besides, if this is the place Pete's being stored, why would we want to line their pockets?'

'We don't know he's being stored here.'

'But if he is.'

'Then that's another story.'

'Another story? You want *another* story? Isn't this one bad enough?'

We were wondering what to do while waiting for the Magic Joke Shop to open – if it opened while we were actually *in* Wonkton – when the rain started. Heavy rain that looked like getting heavier.

'Better get under cover,' Angie said.

'Where?'

'I don't know. There?'

She meant Wax Works, the wax museum next door. Well, we had to go somewhere. But when I saw how much it cost to get in – two arms and legs, not wax ones either – I said I'd rather get wet.

Angie frowned. 'What are you, McCue, an accountant all of a sudden?'

In we went.

The woman at the ticket desk was not the life and soul of the party. Probably never had been, even at parties. It was the hatchet face that did it. The kind of hatchet that's chopped too much firewood on cold winter mornings. No eye contact, no smiles, definitely no jokes.

There were only two other actual living people in the museum at first – Golden Oldie holiday-makers, you could tell by their shorts – but they were already on their way out so then it was just us. Us and the wax figures. Most of the waxes looked more alive than the woman at the ticket desk.

I liked the superheroes, like the Hulk, Spiderman, the X-Men and X-Ladies, and the fairy tale characters were quite cool – Snow White, Little Red Riding Hood, the Three Bears, all that crew. And there were famous actors, and pop stars, and kings and queens, and a lot of people I didn't know, like politicians and scientists. We didn't like to speak near some of the ones we didn't know in case they were actually real and just pausing for thought. I wanted to go down to the Chamber of Horrors, where they kept the murderers and torture chambers and the execution gear, but Angie wasn't keen and I didn't fancy going down by myself, so we stayed up top.

Parts of the place were quite organised but other parts weren't, unless I missed it. I mean, you didn't get all the musicians together, or all the TV gardeners and TV room designers and TV chefs and TV newsreaders, but there were little groups dotted about with these big screaming signs over them telling us that they were ASTRONAUTS or

CHARACTERS FROM DICKENS or GUNSLINGERS OF THE OLD WEST and so on. We were tootling past a bunch of short wax figures by a giant toadstool (no big screaming sign here) when I noticed a small door behind them. The short wax figures were dwarves, but the door was ajar.

'Think we're meant to go through there?' I said.

'Not unless the notice was put there for a laugh,' Angie said.

'What notice?'

She pulled me aside. Where I'd been standing before, a dwarf's hat blocked the notice on the door. The notice said *Strictly No Entry*. 'Oh, that notice,' I said. But because it said *Strictly No Entry* I suddenly needed to see what was on the other side, so I stepped round the dwarves – 'S'cuse me, s'cuse me, s'cuse me' – and peered through the ajar bit of the door.

'Ange.'

'What?'

'Here.'

She also stepped round the dwarves, but she didn't say excuse me. Together we looked through the ajar part.

'Well, how about that,' Angie said.

We were looking into Striker's Magic Joke Shop.

'Must be owned by the same people,' I said. 'If we'd gone into the shop we could have snuck through this door to here and not paid.'

Angie stared at me wide-eyed. 'Jiggy McCue, you are getting so *tight*.' But she liked the idea, you could tell.

Still, we were in the museum now, and we'd paid, so we had to get our money's worth. We carried on looking round.

When we came to a black curtain with the words NIGHTMARE CREATURES beside it we didn't go in right away. 'After you,' I said to Angie, because I'm polite like that.

She went in. The black curtain dropped behind her. I waited. No scream, so I went in too. It was dark in there. Not absolutely dark because there was a bit of light from a door at the far side of the room, but dark enough.

'BOO!'

I almost pulled the curtain down with me.

'Don't do that!'

'You'd have done it if you'd had the nerve to

come in first,' Angie said in the almost total darkness.

'No, I wouldn't.' But she was right. I would've.

Spooky music played quietly while I hung near the entrance till my eyes got used to the light shortage. Soon I could make out phoney bats flapping slowly on the ceiling, and cobwebs, and ghostly tree-shapes, but this was just background stuff. It was the figures that made you gulp. There were ten or twelve of them, a bit taller than life-size, most of them, with eyes that glowed in the dark and seemed to be watching us. They had little illuminated signs by their feet to tell you who they were, but you didn't want to stoop to read them because the NIGHTMARE CREATURES would be towering over you then, so you screwed your eyes up to read them. I knew some of them even without the name tags – Dracula, The Mummy, Freddy Krueger, Frankenstein's Monster, a few others – but the rest were new to me. I'd never heard of The Voodoo Queen of New Orleans, for instance, or The Gargoyle of Cruel Castle, or Rhama the Living Corpse. I wouldn't want to meet any of *them* on a dark night. Bad enough in a dark room.

I was standing next to a terrifically realistic Wolf Man wondering if I dared touch his fur when a hand gripped my arm. Now, in case you wonder, standing in a dark room next to a huge hairy man with teeth like nail scissors while weird music plays isn't what you want to be doing when a hand grips your arm. I didn't make a sound. I didn't *have* a sound. But my hair jerked to the kind of attention it wouldn't normally jerk to unless a high-voltage electric cable had suddenly plugged itself into my bottom without a licence.

But it was just Angie's hand, trying to attract my attention. 'Jig. Look there.'

I could just about see that she was pointing at the door on the other side of the room. The exit. Like the entrance, the exit had a black curtain over it, except the exit curtain was caught up at the side, probably when the last people left in a hurry, screaming. All I could see through the exit was another bunch of waxworks in the next part of the museum.

'What am I looking at?'

Instead of telling me she grabbed my arm again. This time my hair stayed down. 'See you around,'

I said to Wolf Man as I followed my arm to the exit.

'Next full moon,' he growled. But maybe I imagined that.

The light was dazzling outside the NIGHTMARE CREATURES room and I blunk like a maniac as Angie dragged me to the waxworks I'd seen from inside. When we stopped and I could see properly again I read the big sign over the group. ORDINARY PEOPLE, it screamed.

'Ordinary people?' I said. 'I see ordinary people every day, on the estate, at school, at home, the shops, everywhere. Why would I want to see them in a museum?'

'Look,' Angie said. Her voice sounded kind of strange, like it was going to snap or something.

I scanned the ORDINARY PEOPLE. There was a woman in a suit with a briefcase (I mean a woman with a briefcase in a suit) (no, that doesn't sound right either, but never mind), a man holding a glass of beer, an old dear in a wheelchair, a teacher, a bricklayer with a bit of brick wall, and quite a few others, all terrifically ordinary. I wondered why anyone would pay a real arm and a real leg to see people no different from themselves in wax. Maybe the museum had run out of ideas. Couldn't think of any more celebrities, historical characters or whatever.

'So this is what ORDINARY PEOPLE look like,' I said.

'Why are you shouting?' Angie asked.

'I'm not shouting, I'm just saying what the sign says.'

'You haven't looked at that one.'

'Which one?'

She pointed to a schoolboy sitting at a desk, staring into space like we do all the time at our school, Ranting Lane. He wore a school uniform and his tie was loose and wonky, the way we like it and the teachers don't. His jacket was half off one shoulder, a bottle of pop stuck out of one of the pockets, his shirt hung out, his shoelaces were undone, shoes were dirty, and a wax rat peeped out of the bulging schoolbag on the floor. He was as ordinary as any boy you could trip over in the playground, but I saw why Angie wanted me to look at him.

'Looks a bit like Pete,' I said.

'A bit?' Angie said. 'It's exactly like him.'

'Well, there's a likeness, but look at the nose. Pete's nose isn't that shape.'

'Oh, you're an expert on the shape of Garrett's nose now, are you?'

'I've grown up with Garrett's nose,' I said. 'That nose has always been there, usually poking into my business. I know that nose almost as well as my own. Better actually, 'cos I see his from all angles.'

She wasn't having it. 'It's only because this one's not flesh and blood that it looks different.'

'OK then, the eyes. Pete's eyes aren't green.'

'Who says his eyes aren't green?'

Now that she mentioned it I wasn't totally sure. I mean you look at people's eyes all the time, but you don't often remember the colour afterwards. Well, if they're very dark you might notice. Or very pale. Or very bloodshot. But most eyes are just eyes.

'His hair's darker,' I said. 'Pete's hair is definitely darker.'

'It's the light in here.'

'I really don't think it's a waxwork of Pete, Ange. They couldn't have made a complete waxwork in the time.'

'I didn't say it was a waxwork of Pete,' she said.

I stared, first at her, then back at the wax.

'You think this is the *real* Pete? The *actual* Pete?'

'Yes. I do. I think this is where Neville's been keeping him.'

'This isn't exactly non-existence,' I said.

'Being on display in a museum is existence?' she said.

'Well…no. Not much of one anyway.'

'The museum people – or the magic joke shop people – must be in cahoots with Neville,' she said. 'It's the only explanation. Unless…'

'Unless what?'

'Unless Neville didn't have anything to do with this. Unless the museum or magic joke shop people snatched Pete because they needed an extra waxwork and Nev took the credit so we'd help him get his size back.'

I still wasn't convinced this was Pete, but now that she'd put the idea in my head the wax figure made me nervous. I walked round it, looked down at it from all sides and angles. There were things about it that didn't look too Petey to me, but maybe it was the light like Angie had said, or the wax. It looked real enough. Like a kid just sitting there, very still, pretending to be blank. Like he might turn his head any second, say something sarcastic. I noticed the hand on the desk. It was holding a pen and the point of the pen rested on a school exercise book where it had made a shape like this.

↯

'Interesting,' I said.

'What is?'

'That. The doodle. Remind you of anything?'

Angie peered. 'Should it?'

'How about lightning?'

She shrugged. 'I suppose. At a stretch.'

I fished in my pocket for the card that had landed in my trainer at Devil's Bridge. I checked it to be sure, then handed it to her. She looked at it. At the Striker's Magic Joke Shop logo. Lightning.

'You think Pete managed to make the doodle before he came over all waxy?' she said. 'As a clue for us to find if we came in here?'

'You tell me, you're the one who thinks this *is* Pete.'

'Well, if the card did come from him it's the second time he's pointed us towards the shop.'

'The shop which is just the other side of that door back there,' I said.

'Yes,' she said. 'Hey, maybe there's some sort of antidote there. In the shop.'

'Antidote?'

'Some kind of dewaxer. Something that will turn this – him – back into flesh-and-blood Pete.'

'If there is such a thing, what are the chances it'll be just sitting there waiting to be found?'

'Slim,' she said.

'Anorexic,' I said.

'But if we can find it we can get Pete back without resizing Neville, and Neville will be small-fry forever and the world will be saved from his missssh!'

'Saved from his missssh?' I repeated, before noticing the finger she'd put over her lips. A pair of parents had come in with a little boy and girl who immediately started running round pointing at the ORDINARY PEOPLE.

'Don't touch, Katy,' said the mother as Katy stuck an elbow in the wax fireman's stomach.

Katy giggled and ran through the curtain to the NIGHTMARE CREATURES room. Nothing happened for about ten seconds, then there was this ear-shattering screech and Katy flew out with her mouth almost as big as her face.

'Katy, what happened?' the mother said.

Katy didn't say. She rushed round the corner to another part of the museum. Her mother rushed after her. So did her father. The little boy didn't. He didn't go anywhere. He came and stood with Ange and me. Grinned up at us like an old pal and...poked wax Pete in the chest.

'Don't do that,' Angie said.

The kid grinned broader still and poked Pete harder. Angie put a gentle hand on the boy's shoulder. Smiled down at him.

'If you touch him again,' she said, 'you'll be turned into wax like him, and you'll stay here forever and ever and ever, amen.'

The boy spun round and raced after his family.

Angie bent over the Garretty waxwork. 'Pete,' she said. 'If you can hear me, we're going to save you.'

'Can wax hear?' I wondered.

'He might not be all wax.'

'The only unwax bit he needs to hear you is an

258

ear,' I said, 'and those ears look pretty waxy to me. Mind you, Garrett's earholes looked pretty waxy even before he got the full treatment.'

'One for all and all for lunch, Pete,' Angie whispered in a wax lug. Then she took her mother's camera out of her pocket.

'What are you doing?'

'Taking a picture, whadda ya think?'

'Of his ear?'

'Of Pete.'

'But we've got stacks of pictures of Pete.'

'Not as a waxwork, we haven't.'

'So…you want a souvenir?'

'It's not for me, dumbo, it's evidence.'

'Evidence?'

'For the police. To show what they've done to Pete.'

I pointed to a sign on the wall.

NO PHOTOGRAPHY

'This is important,' she said.

She aimed the camera and clicked the shutter. The automatic flash was so blinding even the waxworks almost blinked. She popped the camera back in her pocket, then, casual as you like, taking in waxes as we went in case a hidden CCTV camera was following our every move, we returned to the connecting door we'd seen earlier. We hesitated before going through. We had no idea what might be on the other side. Might be someone waiting to pounce on us and turn us into wax. If they did that, what would they do with us? Put us on display next to Pete? Bung us behind a wall so no one would ever find us? Five minutes from now we too could find ourselves removed from existence. But we had no choice. We had to do this thing.

Angie and I took deep breaths, one each. Then I followed her through the door marked *Strictly No Entry*.

Chapter Twenty

There were no lights on in the shop because it wasn't open, and there was no one waiting for us, but that didn't stop us being edgy. We tiptoed round as quiet as pickled mice, using hand-signals, mouth-shapes and eyebrows to communicate. Trotting through that shadowy, silent shop, where you could turn any corner and find a screech-worthy horror mask staring at you, I'd rather have been locked in the NIGHTMARE CREATURES room without a torch or sandwich.

It was hard to tell where the jokes stopped and the magic began in Striker's Magic Joke Shop. It wasn't a huge shop, but like the museum it went off in all directions, and everywhere you looked there was joke and magic stuff. You don't need me to tell you the kind of things you find in a shop like that, but here's a few anyway.

Celebrity masks, celebrity wigs, fake sick, rubber chickens, funny T-shirts, chattering teeth, bad disguises and magic wands. The actual jokes, mostly in sealed envelopes, included animal jokes, blonde jokes, sports jokes, doctor-doctor jokes and teacher-teacher jokes. There were practical jokes too, like stink bombs, fake winning lottery tickets, fake bullet holes, hot toilet paper, burping beer mugs, a creeping hand, a running rat, wacky teeth, vampire teeth, naughty door signs, a swearing punch bag (I wanted to try that one but didn't dare), funny fridge magnets and two-headed coins. In the 'Magic Tricks and Illusions' section there were things like The Hanky That Changes Colour, The Disappearing Ball, Magic Handcuffs, Magic Linking Rings, The Electric Card Deck, Multiplying Rabbits, and A Ton Of Other Things I Can't Be Bothered To Mention.

OK, that's the description out of the way. Now I'll tell you what we found there. We found...

Nothing.

Nothing that would haul Pete out of the wax anyway. After about ten minutes' sloping silently round the shop expecting someone to come in any minute and catch us, we gave up. It might have helped if we'd had some idea what we were looking for, but we didn't. There was certainly no magic dewaxing wand or anything like that. We started towards the door we'd come in by, but just before we got to it Angie gripped me by the bulging bicep and told me to 'Stay here!' in silent mouth language while she went back for something.

While I was waiting I took in a nearby display cabinet full of dolls. I don't spend a lot of time looking at dolls, but there wasn't anything else, and besides, these weren't dolly-wolly dolls for dear little girls with dear little prams. There was a policeman doll, a burglar doll, a fireman doll, a farmer doll, a lady jogger doll, a tramp doll, a builder doll, a nurse doll, an air-hostess doll, a doctor doll, a pirate doll, a spaceman doll, and a devil doll. Yes, a devil doll. That one was a surprise. What was even more of a surprise was that he didn't look the least bit devilish. He had the standard devil kit on – red cloak and boots, black shirt and trousers, and he was holding a toy trident like the one Neville wanted us to find – but he didn't look very evil. Didn't look evil at all. With his fat side-whiskers and jolly grin he looked like a happy farmer in fancy dress. He was also cheaper than the rest. There was a little notice by his feet which said 'Storm Damaged'. I wondered what a storm had to do with the burn mark in his shirt. Maybe someone dropped a cigarette on it, I thought. Some storm.

When Angie came back she was carrying something. A Combo Fun Box. I was shocked. I would have asked about this, but she rushed me to the exit before I could speak. We looked round the door before going into the museum. There were people the other side, eyeing the dwarves. We waited till they'd gone, then stepped through. Now I could ask my question.

'You *took* that?'

Angie looked offended. 'Of course I didn't take it. I paid for it.'

'Oh, and who did you pay, the Inflatable Serving Person?'

'I left the money by the till. Had to leave more than it's worth actually, because I didn't have the right amount. You owe me half.'

'On your bike,' I said. 'I'm not paying half for something you didn't even ask me about.'

'Oh yes you are, Jiggy McCue.'

'We'll discuss it when you're asleep. Why have you got it? You said you might buy it as a welcome home present. He's not home yet.'

'I thought we could show it to him while we're here. It might get him excited enough to come back to us.'

'Shake off the wax, you mean?'

Now that she heard it in actual words rather than in her head she looked pretty doubtful herself.

'Doesn't seem very likely, does it?'

'Not very, no.'

We returned to the group of ORDINARY PEOPLE. There were a few visitors there too now, so we hung around pretending to look at things until they pushed off. Then we went to where the wax schoolboy was sitting.

'Pete,' Angie whispered. 'I don't know if you can hear me but we've got The Combo Fun Box for you. Look.'

She held the box in front of the waxy eyes. They didn't blink. There was no sign of life in them.

'If you come back to us you can open it,' she said. 'You can be a real pest with all the things inside. We won't mind. We'll put up with it. Think of the fun

265

you can have playing terrible jokes on people.'

Still nothing in the wax eyes.

'Not working,' I said.

'I'm going to open it,' Angie said. 'There might be something inside that he won't be able to resist.'

She pulled the lid off. Inside were all the things described on the box and a lot more. Angie chose the bloody bandaged finger with the nail through it. While I held the box she slipped it over her own finger, then turned round and waggled it in front of the wax peepers.

Not a flicker.

She dipped in again. This time she put on one of the moustaches and the pair of giant latex lips. If she'd turned round unexpectedly and looked at me with those things on I would have collapsed in hysterics, but the waxwork she thought was Pete didn't react at all.

'Still not working,' I said.

She whipped the moustache and lips off. 'I just haven't found the right thing,' she said, picking through the box for something else.

'Oh not the squirting flower,' I said when she took it out.

'Keep your voice down. We won't jolt him out of this if he knows what's coming.'

'Don't you have to fill it first?'

'No, it's not the water squirting type.'

She pinned the plastic flower to her coat and also put on a pair of bloodshot eyeballs on springs. 'Hi, Pete,' she said in a comic voice as she turned. 'Like a sniff of my flower?'

As she said, 'Like a sniff of my flower?' she leaned towards him and squeezed the rubber pump thing on the tube that dangled from it. A bubble of green slime burst out and hit the waxy face a second before a sharp voice behind us asked us what we thought we were playing at.

We spun round. The hatchet-faced woman from the ticket desk was standing there. I shoved The Combo Fun Box behind me and stepped away so she would think that maybe, just maybe, I had nothing to do with this. When Angie said, 'It was an accident' even I wanted to say, 'Oh yeah?'

'Accident!' Hatchet-face said, storming towards us.

'We were just – '

'*She* was just,' I said.

' – standing here and this sort of...happened.'

The woman glared from Angie to wax Pete to Angie again.

'So why are you wearing that?'

She meant the flower. Angie looked down at it. The bloodshot eyeballs on springs looked too.

'My mother gave it to me.'

'Your mother, eh? Where is she? I'd like a word.'

'She's not with us. Don't you remember us when we came in? We were on our own.'

'I can't be expected to remember everyone,' hatchet-face replied, like there'd been armies of people in, not just us and half a dozen others. 'Do you have any idea how valuable these waxworks are? Don't move!'

She rushed out. We just stood there. Like waxworks. She was back almost immediately with a cloth, which she started to wipe Pete's face with, very gently like it was a baby's bottom.

'And please take those things off!'

Angie took off the bloodshot eyeballs on springs.

'What's that you've got there?'

Hatchet-face was looking at me.

'Got where?'

'Behind your back.'

'Nothing.'

'Show me.'

I brought The Combo Fun Box out from hiding.

'Where'd you get that?'

'It's hers,' I said. 'Her mother gave it to her. That's where the flower and eyeballs came from. I was just holding it for her.'

Angie focussed on me like a hungry shark suddenly noticing a swimmer. It was a look that said, 'I wish I had jaws wide enough to bite your head off and crunch it up and spit the bits at this woman'. Just as well she'd taken off the eyeballs on springs. You can't give people looks like that with eyeballs on springs.

'If your mother gave you that box,' Hatchet-face said to Angie, 'why have you got it with you in here?' She sounded very suspicious.

'She gave it to me out in the street just before we came in,' Angie said. 'Didn't you see us carrying it when we bought our tickets? Oh, no. You said. You don't remember us.'

'Your mother just bought it, did she?'

'I don't know. S'pose she must have done.'

'And gave it to you without a carrier bag?'

'It was starting to rain. She wanted the bag to cover her head.' Nice one, Ange, I thought.

'I've seen a box like that before,' the woman said. 'In the shop next door. Which is owned by the same person who owns Wax Works.'

We glanced at one another. Just as we thought. The same person owned both shops.

'And the shop next door isn't open yet,' she added. 'So your mother couldn't have bought it this morning.'

'I didn't say she bought it this morning,' Angie said.

'Yes you did.'

'I didn't. I said I *suppose* she bought it this morning. She might have had it for days and just decided to give it to me today, outside. She does things like that, my mum. She's very out of the blue.'

The woman stepped back from wax Pete. The green slime was off his face and on the cloth. Some of it was on her hands.

'Did you take a photo in here a while ago?'

'Photo?' Angie said, looking immediately guilty.

'Our sensors showed a flash about fifteen minutes back. Photography is not allowed in the museum.'

Angie covered the bulge in her pocket. 'Well it wasn't us. We haven't got a camera. Can I ask a question?'

The woman narrowed her eyes. 'You can ask.'

'How long has this waxwork been here?'

'I have no idea. I just mind the desk. There haven't been any new figures since March as far as I know.'

Angie glanced at me. She's lying, the glance said.

'I ought to report you for this,' the woman said.

'Report us? Who to?'

'The police, who do you think?'

'We didn't take a picture,' Angie said fiercely.

'I don't mean that, I mean for what you did to him.'

'I said it was an accident.'

'Yes. So you did.'

'Anyway, I'm sorry.' Angie looked at me again. This time to make sure the woman knew that whatever had been done it was down to both of us, not just her. '*We're* sorry.'

'Well…'

She was weakening. Probably thinking about all the upset if she shopped us to the Bill. The boys and girls in blue swarming all over the place, the interrogation under spotlights, the statement she'd have to make, the court case with mothers in tears and her in the dock giving evidence, the reporters outside her door when she came back from the butcher's, the bad pictures in the tabloids of her showing her knickers as she got out of taxis. So she just asked us to leave. Which we did, gladly. Went out into the rain without even saying goodbye to wax Pete.

Chapter Twentyone

Because it was raining I shoved The Combo Fun Box up my jacket. I caught an eyeful of myself in a shop window as we were passing. I looked like a pregnant robot, so I tried walking like one for a while, all stiff legs and swinging arms, till Angie told me I looked stupid.

Not that we spent a lot of time in the rain. Mostly we went from doorway to doorway to keep out of it, and into a shopping arcade, and when it eased off a bit we hauled ourselves up the hill to Journey's End. When we got there I stood sagging against the wall, feeling that my big square robot chest was going to explode, while Angie went indoors. In a while I followed her in and up. I did not pause for breath outside the Professor's door.

There was no one in our flat, which surprised us. The mothers we knew about, but we couldn't think where the dads might have gone seeing as it was still daytime. I could have phoned Dad on his mobile, but he's old enough to go out without me checking up on him. We got ourselves something to eat, but then, because we didn't know what else to do, we mostly just sat there, sighing into our hands.

'Looks like we'll have to go the Nev route after all,' Angie said.

'Find the trident, you mean?'

'Find the trident, hand it over, watch him grow big and even meaner. It's the only way he'll dewax Pete for us.'

'You still think that waxwork was Pete?'

'Yes. Absolutely.'

'Well even if it is, even if doing what Neville wants is the only way we'll get him back, we still have no idea where to look for the trident.'

'No. Small snag, that.'

She opened The Combo Fun Box and started going through it for something to do. I went to the window. The rain was coming down hard again. What a holiday, I thought. First we don't go to the place we were looking forward to, then we meet my old enemy Neville the Devil, then we lose Pete and have to spend all our time trying to get him back.

Then it rains.

'Heeeeeeeey. Jig. Here.'

I turned from the window. 'What do you think I am, a pet dog?'

'Here, boy, here!'

I scampered to her. She was holding a small blue bottle from The Combo Fun Box, screwing her eyes up to read the label.

'What's that?'

'I can't make out everything it says, but...Jig, I think this is it.'

'Is what?'

'Neville's resizer.'

'What? No. Neville's resizer is a trident. He said so.'

'He didn't say it was an *actual* trident.'

She pointed to the name of the manufacturer on the box lid. I gaped. The name of the manufacturer was Trident Humour Products™. It had been under our noses the whole time. I looked closer at the 'fun' things in the box. Every one had a tiny little trident symbol on it.

'All Trident products,' Angie said. 'A whole box of them. But this, I'm sure, *this* is the one Neville needs.'

She meant the small blue bottle.

'Why that?'

'Because of what it says on the label. That a few drops of Hiagra will make selected Trident Humour Products grow and grow.'

'Hiagra?'

'That's what it's called. Hi as in height, I guess.'

'Neville's not a Trident Humour Product.'

'No, but he must have discovered that Hiagra will do it for him too. Give him back his height. His size.'

'Then all we have to do is take this to him, sprinkle a few drops on him, and there is, large as life and twice as ugly, and we get Pete back.'

'Yeh. Let's go downstairs.'

'He might not be in.'

'I don't know where else he'd be. Not on the beach in this.'

'The Prof'll probably be there too. What then?'

'I don't know. We chat, I suppose.'

'What about? The weather?'

She put the little bottle in her pocket and we went down to the flat below. We knocked on the door. A small voice on the other side said, 'If it's who I think it is, come in. If it isn't, hoppit.'

We opened the door. Neville was standing on the other side. We looked around. No one else there, just some of the smaller props from the show and the boxes the puppets were kept in.

'Where's the Prof?'

'He's not here,' Neville said.

'Where is he?'

'You don't need to know.'

'He's gone to the shop,' said a tiny voice.

Angie went to the box she thought the voice had come from and lifted the lid. Her eyes popped.

'I thought you said he was away on a course,' she said to Neville.

I went to look. The puppet in the box was Mr Punch. And he was just lying there. No sign of life at all.

'You also said he wasn't actually a puppet,' I said.

'He been telling you porkies?' said Judy, kicking the lid off the box next door and sitting up.

'What's this all about?' Angie demanded.

Neville sighed. 'OK, OK, I was having you on. Punch isn't alive, he never was alive, there are no plans to make him alive. All right?'

'Punch alive!' said Judy. 'Now that *would* be a turn up!'

'So the Professor didn't send him away?' I said.

'No, he just stopped taking him out of his box. There's no place for angry puppets at a tinpot resort like Wonkton and Punch couldn't suddenly become Mr Nicey-Nicey, his face is too well-known.'

'That's why the Professor took *him* on,' Judy said. 'Desperate, he was.'

'I should have brought Punch to life instead of you,' Neville said.

Judy folded her arms and went all hoity-toity. 'I don't know why you didn't, if you feel like that.'

'I'll tell you why I didn't, dough-head. If I'd brought Mr Punch to life he'd probably have beaten me up for my trouble. That puppet's a psycho.'

'You'll be glad of my company when you're on the scrap heap,' Judy said. 'Be laughing on the other side of your fence then, you will.'

'Face,' Neville said. 'Other side of my face. Cretinous old bat.'

'What's this about the scrap heap?' Angie asked.

'The Professor's closing the show,' he replied.

'Well I know he's thinking of it. It's not definite, though.'

'It wasn't. Is now. He's made up his mind.'

'What made him decide to go ahead?'

'Today's weather. The rain. It was all getting on top of him without this. Forced to put on a crummy show like Mr Nicey-Nicey and Ms Sweet after years of good wholesome family entertainment full of gratuitous violence and shouting, then, today, bucketing down so he can't open at all. Final straw.'

'By the weekend we'll be redundant,' Judy chipped in.

'So I really need that trident,' Neville said. 'Without it, I'll be on a park bench with an eggcup of whisky in a little brown bag. Either that or sitting next to her in an Oxfam shop waiting to be picked up by some snot-nosed brat who thinks I'm adorable. Have you got it? Tell me you've got it.'

'We've got it,' Angie said.

'You're just saying that.'

'No, we've got it. Really.'

He became suspicious. 'How?'

'Never you mind. Do you want it or don't you?'

'I want it. Where is it?'

'Say please,' I said.

He squinted at me. 'Now why would I say a thing like that?'

'Because then we might give you what you want.'

'You'll give it to me anyway because you want your friend back.'

'Still be nice to hear a please.'

'Nev the Dev don't do nice.'

'Say it anyway. For me.'

'I can't. It would be rude.'

'Rude?'

'P.l.e.a.s.e. is a six-letter word where I come from.'

'It's a six-letter word here too,' I said, counting the letters.

'Yeah, but where I'm from it's a dirty six-letter word.'

'Where he's from!' cried Judy. 'He does talk nonsense.'

'Seal the plug-hole, simpleton!'

'Oh, let's just get it over with,' Angie said in exasperation.

She took the little bottle out of her pocket and held it up.

'What's that?' said Neville.

'The height cure.'

'We finally realised you didn't mean an actual trident,' I said.

'*I* finally realised,' said Angie.

'You meant a Trident product. This Trident product.'

'Which makes things grow,' said Angie.

'Which'll make *you* grow,' I said.

Neville sat down with a bump on the floor.

'I should have expected it. Brains like mushy peas.'

'Isn't it what you wanted?' Angie asked.

'Ha!'

'But look.' I snatched the bottle from her. 'The trident on the label, the words saying it makes things grow. It has to be it.'

'It was it,' Neville said.

'Was it?' said Angie.

'It's the stuff I used the first time. It only works once.'

I gasped. 'Are you saying you started life the size you are now?'

'There!' screeched Judy. 'The truth is out! They know!'

'All right,' Neville said. 'I started out as a doll. Satisfied?'

'You started out as a *doll*?' I said. 'A *live* doll?'

'I wasn't live to begin with. I was like the others. Just another dumb plaything. Until something happened.'

'What something?'

'Something like a dark and stormy night. I was in the attic over the shop with the other new dolls waiting to be put in the display cabinet downstairs. The skylight was open. Lightning kerpowed through the gap and splatted me. Right here.' He touched his chest. 'It was like switching a light on, but more painful. Some awakening. My chest hurt for days.'

'Frankenstein all over again,' Angie said.

'Who?' said Neville.

'Forget it. What happened then?'

'Matter of fact I went a little crazy. Suddenly, from a doll-faced moron that didn't even say 'Mama' or wet itself when tilted I had full consciousness and physicality. Also, being a devil doll I had devilish powers. Just little powers, but still powers, and lemme tell you it felt *great*! I hopped down the stairs

282

to the shop and ran around clicking my heels and wa-hooing. The one thing that stopped me turning the place to rubble with joy was the heather. There was a vase of it on the counter. Heather does stuff to me. You may remember that.'*

'When did you stop being doll-sized?' Angie asked.

'Hold the impatience, I'm telling my life-story here. First off, I took against the devil costume I was born in. Outside of the shop who would take me seriously in naff gear like that? Also, there was a very uncool lightning burn in the shirt. So I switched duds with one of the dolls on a shelf. I've worn his ever since.' He twirled around with his little arms in the air. 'Neat, huh?'

'This shop,' I said. 'It's not in Wonkton, is it?'

'Of course it's in Wonkton. Why'd you think I'm here? Why'd you think *you're* here? Why'd you think I sent you the card that goes with the shop as a clue?'

'So it was you who sent the card. And the shop is…'

I glanced at Angie, who was already glancing at me.

---

* Sorry about this, but if you want to know about Neville and heather and don't know already, you'll just have to read *The Killer Underpants*.

'I was reeling from the heather,' Neville went on, 'and I backed into a shelf and knocked over a bottle of that stuff. The lid must have been loose because it splashed my hand and I started to grow. All over. It was kinda scary. In five minutes, ten, I was small human size. Handy that the clothes grew with me, or I don't know what I'd have done.'

'So it worked on you even though the label said it only works on Trident Humour Products,' Angie said.

'I am a Trident Humour Product,' said Neville.

'You're what?'

'You want it in Japanese, German and Outer Mongolian? I'm a Trident Humour Product. Was, that is. Originally.'

'Me too,' said Judy.

'Don't remind me,' he snarled. 'That makes us almost related.' He turned back to us. 'It's not meant to work on all T.H.P.'s so I was as surprised as anyone when it grew me.'

'How do you know it'll only work once?' Angie asked.

'Didn't you read the small print?' said Neville.

'I tried. Didn't have a magnifying glass.'

'Well take it from me. That's why I need the trident.'

'So you really did mean a proper trident. But how do you know it'll do what Hiagra can't?'

'I don't. But I was holding it when the lightning hit and I left it behind when I quit the shop to start my life in the outside world. I'm hoping the trident still contains some of the devilish energy that woke me. If it doesn't I'm stuck this way.'

'This trident,' I said. 'How big is it?'

'How big? It's for a person the size I am now, what do you think? It was my trident when I was a doll. I dumped it along with the nerdy dev costume before I got heightened, so it stayed small like the rest of my old gear.'

'And you left it with the doll you switched clothes with?'

'Yeah. The laughing bozo with the cheek hair.'

'I've seen it then,' I said.

'You've seen my trident?'

'Yes. I thought it was a toy.'

'It *was* a toy,' Neville said. 'Like I was.'

'You didn't tell us to look for a toy.'

'When did you see it?' he demanded.

'This morning. In the Magic Joke Shop.'

'Impossible,' he said. 'The Magic Joke Shop wasn't open this morning.'

'We snuck through from the wax museum. There's a secret sort of door.'

'Ah. But you didn't...see anyone?'

'No. Just as well or we'd have been in trouble.'

'You saw the trident,' said Angie in disbelief. 'You saw the trident we've been looking absolutely everywhere for and you didn't think to mention it?'

'I didn't know we were looking for a *toy*,' I said through my teeth.

'Unbelievable. Still, at least we know where it is now. We can go down and get it later. If they're open.'

'To get the trident we'll have to buy the doll Neville switched clothes with,' I pointed out.

'Did you notice the price?' she asked.

'It was the cheapest of the lot because of the burn hole in the shirt, but it's still more than I want to pay for something I'll chuck in the bin first chance I get.'

'We'll buy it between us.'

'If we do I'll add it to what Pete owes for all the loot I'm laying out to get him back.'

Angie gave me one of her best withering looks. I withered.

'You've told us a bunch of lies,' she said to Neville.

'Porkie pies,' said Judy. 'He tells them all the time.'

'Well, you might as well tell us the rest now. Not lies. The truth.'

'You don't want the truth,' he said. 'It's not that interesting.'

'Give it a whirl. We'll try to be fascinated.'

'Okey-dokey. When I lost my height I headed back to Wonkton for the trident. It was my only hope of – '

'How did you get here anyway?' I asked. 'How did you even get up to surface level?'*

Neville screwed his face up at the memory. 'It was a long and smelly journey and I don't want to relive it. Now will there be any more interruptions or can I get on? I hate being interrupted.'

'Sorry.'

'OK. Just don't do it again please.'

---

* Another detail from *The Killer Underpants*. Don't blame me, blame Neville. I didn't ask him to come back and bore you rigid with this stupid story. Jig.

'You said it!' Angie cried.

'Said what?' said Neville.

'Please.'

'I did not.'

'I thought please was a dirty word where you come from.'

'It is. I didn't say it.'

'You did,' I said.

'I didn't.'

'He did, didn't he?' Angie said to Judy.

Judy folded her hands across her tum and nodded. 'He did.'

'You come from the attic over Striker's Magic Joke Shop,' I said. 'How can it be a dirty word in an attic?'

'It's a dirty attic. Now what do you say I sing a little song, or tell some jokes, or stand on my head maybe? I might as well, seeing as you obviously don't want to hear my story.'

'OK. Tell it.'

'When I got back to Wonkton I snuck into the shop to look for the trident. It was night again, but much easier getting in than getting out the time before. When I left I was so big I had to break a window. This time I got in through the cat flap.'

288

'You're lucky the cat didn't get you,' Angie said.

'No problem. It was stuffed. But Striker caught me.'

'Striker?' said Judy. She sounded surprised.

'Mr Striker. Whose shop it is.'

He glared at her, as if daring her to say another word. She didn't, but she looked as if she wanted to.

'I bet he was surprised to see a walking-talking doll,' Angie said.

'Ex-doll,' said Neville. 'He wasn't too surprised. It's a magic shop. Weird stuff goes on down there.'

'Did you tell him you needed the trident?'

'Oh, I told him. No dice. Striker is not a nice man. He's very big, and he only has one arm, and he's got a huge black beard and he growls a lot. Terrifies the customers.'

Judy cackled. We didn't bother to ask what was so funny.

'So Striker's the one you called your worst enemy,' I said. 'The devilish type who could turn you to dust with a flick of his fingers. The real reason you brought us all the way here was that you couldn't get the trident yourself.'

'You got it, Wiggy.'

'Jiggy.'

'Nothing to do with us being the ones who turned you back into a doll then,' Angie said.

'I AM NOT A DOLL!' Neville shouted.

'I mean doll size.'

He straightened his bowler, which had slipped over one ear during the shout. 'I might not have thought of you at all if I hadn't dreamt about you one night in my box.'

'You dreamt about us?' I said. 'All three of us?'

'All three, but you most of all. The ringleader.'

'Ringleader?' Angie said. 'Him? Don't make me laugh.'

'When I woke up I was fuming all over again about what you did to me and thinking how sweet revenge would be.'

'So you thought you'd ruin our holiday,' I said.

'Best idea I had since I got back here.'

'We thought you must have had an accomplice who switched the car park signs and made us late for the plane,' said Angie.

'The hairy hippy who offered us the holiday flat,' I added.

'You were right,' said Neville.

'We were?'

'Yeah. Break open the champagne.'

'Who is he?' Angie asked.

'Mr Woodstock from upstairs.'

'He lives upstairs?'

Neville nodded. 'He saw me running around a few days after I moved in with the Professor. He thought he was hallucinating till I bit his ankle.'

'How did you get him to come all the way to the airport, switch the signs and give us the keys to his flat?'

'I turned his budgie into a wasp, which stung him and flew away. I said I'd do the same to him if he didn't do exactly what I told him. I also swore him to secrecy so I wouldn't get in trouble with the Prof.'

'Where's this Mr Woodstock now?' I said.

'In JoyWorld. Just for the week. I believe he's having a really good time. Sun's always shining. Plenty to do. No chance of getting bored. You ought to go there sometime.'

'How did you get to work for the Professor?' Angie asked.

'I was still in the shop when he came in the day

after I got back,' Nev said. 'Striker was trying to decide whether to sell me to the circus or put me in a baguette with chutney. The Prof happened to be looking for a politically correct puppet to take over from that has-been Punch and Striker did a deal, money changed hands, and I became a slave to Armitage Shanks, Puppet Master.'

'Tee-hee-hee!' said Judy. 'Pinch of salt time! Pinch of sea salt!'

We ignored her. Things were getting clearer. Just a couple more things and we'd know everything.

'Why couldn't you say the trident was at the shop?' I asked. 'And which shop?'

'I sent you the business card, didn't I?' Neville said.

'But why didn't you just come out with it? Why all the mystery?'

'I didn't want to make it too easy for you.'

'Even though you were desperate to get your hands on it?'

'Even though. I wanted to see you run around. I wanted you to have a hard time, like you gave me.'

He paused, then looked at us, one after the other. 'How did I do?'

'Not bad for an ex-doll,' I said.

'What about Pete?' Angie said.

'Pete?' said Neville.

'Our friend. Who you turned to wax.'

'I did *what*?'

'It's no good pretending. We've seen him. You might as well admit it.'

'You want me to admit that I turned your pal to wax?'

'Yes.'

'I didn't turn him to wax,' he said. 'It was Striker.'

'Mr Striker turned Pete to wax?'

'Yup. Don't ask me how. He has his ways.'

'But why?'

'He needed a new waxwork for the museum. He saw your chum, thought, "Hey, just the ticket for a moron school kid waxwork", and did the biz.'

'The woman at the desk said none of the waxes are new,' Angie said.

'Who, Gloria? You don't want to pay any attention to Gloria. She knows less than that one there.'

He meant Judy. Judy stuck her little nose in the air.

'So how do we get him back?' I asked.

'There's only one way,' Neville said.

'What's that?'

'Get me the trident. When you bring me the trident I'll get my size and full powers back, and before I go off into the world to have fun I'll drag your pal out of the wax for you.'

'You think you'll be able to do that?'

'Easy as winking.'

He winked. A flower in a nearby vase wilted and dropped all its petals. It was a plastic flower, too.

Chapter Twentytwo

We'd learnt a lot. Everything, we thought. All we had to do now was go to Striker's Magic Joke Shop and buy the doll with the trident.

'It's pouring down,' I said.

I didn't really need to say this. Angie was standing beside me at the bottom of the stairs looking out at the courtyard and her eyeballs were no longer on springs. She too could see the rain smacking the plant pots like bullets.

'We have to go,' she said. 'Rain or no rain.'

'We'll get wet.'

'Yeah, rain does that to people.'

'And it might not be open.'

'We have to go anyway, in case.'

'We can go when the rain stops,' I said.

'By the time it stops, if it does, the shop could be shut again.'

'It's probably shut now.'

'This conversation is starting to go round in circles.'

'It's pouring down,' I said.

In the end we decided to wait a while in case the rain eased off. An hour later we were standing at the big picture window of the flat, still watching the rain. The town was grey, the little bit of sea between the buildings and trees was grey, the sky was grey. It was the kind of day you can't say much about except 'This is a grey day'. Well, you could also say 'It's a wet day' if you wanted, but why bother?

'Hardly worth going now,' I said.

'Shop might still be open,' Angie said.

'If it ever was,' I said.

'I think you're going through a negative phase,' she said.

'No I'm not,' I said.

Fact was, neither of us was keen to go out while it was like this, so we didn't. We were still there, wondering if the rain would ever stop, when the mothers came in. They were not dry. They might have been dryer if they'd had umbrellas or raincoats, but they didn't, so they weren't.

'I need a shower,' Mum said as they tangoed over the threshold.

'Me too,' said Audrey.

'You want to get wetter?' I said. They were drowning the carpet.

'The shower's not big enough for two,' Angie reminded them.

They decided to take it in turns, but when they were still saying, 'You first,' 'After you,' 'No, I insist,' 'Oh, I couldn't,' after half an hour I suggested they go in alphabetically before I started banging my head on the table top. As it turned out even alphabetically wasn't easy. If they went by their first-name initials (Peg and Audrey) Aud would go first, but if they went by their second-name initials (McCue and Mint) Mum would go. Angie suggested that they flip a coin. She was coin-flipping mad today.

'Who's going to flip it?' Audrey said.

'I'll do it,' I said. 'The one who calls right gets the shower first.'

I flipped one of my own coins on to the back of one of my own hands. I looked at it. The coin, I mean. Heads.

'Heads!' the mothers screamed with one voice.

They gave up the shower plan.

The dads came in a bit later. They'd been at a pub since lunchtime, where they'd gone because they couldn't work out how to make cheese on toast, and they'd stayed because of the rain and because there was a bigscreen TV there. They were wet too, but they didn't want a shower. They wanted to change into dry things, rub their hair with towels, and catch up on the sport they'd been missing while watching up-hill egg and spoon races from Stockholm or whatever at the pub.

'We could do with an extra room here so we wouldn't all have to watch that thing,' Mum said.

'You don't have to watch it,' Dad said.

'Can't help but hear it.'

'So cover your ears.'

'I didn't come on holiday to cover my ears.'

'Yes, turn it off, you two,' said Audrey. 'It's not fair to inflict that shouting and screaming on all of us.'

'We're not shouting and screaming,' said Oliver.

'Just give it a rest,' she said.

The box went off. You can see where Angie gets it from.

'All right, what do we do now?' Dad asked.

'We could talk,' Mum said.

'Talk?' My father's eyes swivelled with worry.

'Yes. About what we've all done today.'

'We can sum that up in half a dozen words,' Oliver said. 'Went to pub, had a sandwich, couple of beers, watched TV.'

'That's more than half a dozen,' Angie said.

'Half a dozen or *so*,' said Oliver.

'Jiggy?' Mum said. 'Angie?'

'What?' we said.

'What have you been up to today?'

'We went out,' I said.

'Walked around,' said Angie.

'Came back,' I said.

'In the wet,' said Ange.

'And that's it?'

'Wonkton-on-Sea is not a theme park,' I said.

'You should have come with us,' said Aud.

'We'd have got even wetter then.'

'There was some cover.'

'You still got wet.'

'Yes, but mostly from walking up that sodding hill,' said Mum.

We thought we'd better ask them what the

Wizard World of Harry Hoojah was like. They muttered something about it being 'wizard' but didn't seem to want to say more than that.

'Worth a visit then,' I said.

'Oh yes,' said Audrey.

'Would you go again?'

'Only at gunpoint.'

The TV went back on. No sport this time though. The mothers took charge of the remote.

The rain stopped after tea. The sun didn't appear again, so it was still pretty grey out, but we didn't fancy being stuck indoors with the Golden Oldies all evening.

'Watch the roads,' Mum said as we headed for the door.

'And don't talk to strangers,' said Aud.

We were almost down to the halfway door when the Professor came out. 'Hi, you two,' he said. We let him go down ahead of us because there wasn't room to pass on the stairs without all three of us turning sideways and throwing our arms in the air like Portuguese Stair Dancers.

When we were outside the Professor asked where we were off to. We said we were just strolling around. He said he'd got soaked earlier. We said we had too, and that was about all we could think of to say to one another, but because you couldn't get anywhere without going down the hill we had to go together. It was a quiet walk.

At the foot of the hill there were a couple of ways a person could go, but the Prof went the same way as us, so we had to plod along with him for a bit. When the silence started to get embarrassing, Angie said, 'See you later,' even though we didn't think we were going to see him later, and we stopped to looked in the nearest window, which belonged to a totally fascinating carpet shop.

We waited till the Professor was out of sight before going on. There weren't many people about, so we didn't step off a lot of curbs to get out of their way and risk our lives in the heavy traffic of Wonkton-on-Sea (two pedal bikes and a mini). We had no idea what we'd do when we got to Striker's Magic Joke Shop because we expected it to be closed still. Most of the other shops were closed, and Striker's seemed to like being closed more than any of them, so we weren't prepared for the sign on the inside of the door when we got there.

> Open for Biz, Jokes & Magic
> Yes, really. We're open at last.
> Come in, come in!

We just hung there, looking at the notice, until Angie gripped the handle and pushed the door back. I thought of staying outside to keep watch, but she grabbed one of my wrists and dragged it after her. There's usually a mad jangly bell in these old shops, but there wasn't in this one. Wasn't even a buzzer. We went in so quietly that even we didn't hear us. We were nervous because of what Neville had told us about Mr Striker. If Striker scared Neville the Devil he was definitely someone to watch out for. And look what he'd done to Pete. A man who could turn someone to wax wasn't one you wanted to annoy.

The shop was almost as dark and gloomy as it had been on our last visit, even though it was open this time. There were a couple of small lights on but that was it. It might not have been so bad if there'd been other customers, but there weren't. No one at the counter waiting to serve us either, but we heard someone banging about in a room behind the counter.

Striker!

Angie followed me to the display unit I'd seen the dolls on. They were still there. All of them.

Except one.

'I see no trident,' Angie whispered.

'It's not here,' I whispered back.

'You said it was.'

'It was. Isn't now.'

'Well where is it?'

'Someone must have bought it.'

'But we need that trident. Without it Neville won't be able to get Pete back for us.'

'There's always Eejit Atkins,' I whispered.

'What?'

'For the third Musketeer.'

I shouldn't have said this. Should've known it wouldn't go down well with her right now. When she screwed her fist into a bundle of knuckles as hard as a bumpy cricket ball and thumped my shoulder I couldn't help the yell of pain.

'Hello?'

We turned, slowly, expecting to find a terrible one-armed, heavily-bearded giant of a man scowling at us. Instead...

'You again,' Professor Shanks said. 'You two stalking me?'

'What are you doing here?' Angie asked. Or it might have been me, I'm kind of hazy about this.

'It's my shop,' he said.

'Your shop?' I said. Or it might have been Angie.

'This and the wax museum next door. I've decided to give up the beach show and concentrate on the business. Do it properly for once, take on a couple more staff maybe. Pity you're not local, and older, you could have joined me.'

'But what about Mr Striker?' one of us asked.

'Mr Striker?'

'We thought it was his shop and museum.'

The Professor laughed. 'There is no Mr Striker.'

'Uh?'

'I only call it Striker's Magic Joke Shop because of the logo. Lightning suggests magic and mystery. Lightning strike? Striker?'

No Striker. No terrible man who made Neville quake in his little boots. And we'd thought we had all the answers. Suddenly we were full of questions. Well, three as turned out. Here they are, with the Professor's answers.

Q.   'What's the newest waxwork in the museum?'

A.   'Johnny Depp. Four years old.'

Q.   'There's a waxwork of Johnny Depp aged four?'

A.   'No, the waxwork is four years old.'

Q.   'That's an unusual doll. How much?'

The first and last questions were Angie's. She asked the last one because she was the one who noticed the doll in the devil costume lying beside the till on the counter. The doll with the side whiskers. The one holding Neville's trident.

'Him?' the Professor said. 'I'd just taken him off sale. Part of my sudden resolve to become more businesslike.'

'Off sale? You mean you don't want to sell him?'

'He's been there for months, and even marked down it's obvious he's not going to go. Who'd buy a doll with a burn in his shirt? I wish I knew how that happened.'

'You don't know?' This was me.

'All I can think of is that when Gloria unpacked the consignment he was part of she dropped some fag ash on him. I've told her not to smoke in the shop, but I know she does when I'm not here.'

'Will you sell him to us?' Angie said.

The Prof looked surprised. 'But he's damaged.'

'He has a nice face.'

'Take him. He's all yours.'

'How much?'

'Nothing. Nothing at all. I was about to chuck him out.'

'We must give you something.'

Angie slapped a note on the table. An actual money note.

The Professor smiled. 'Done. My first customers on the day I decided to take this business seriously. Thanks.'

Outside with the doll and trident in a Striker's Magic Joke Shop bag, we set off along the street. What I most wanted to do in all the world was kick Angie six or seven times, quite hard. The reason I didn't was that she would have kicked me back, eight or nine times, and harder.

'You handed money over when you didn't need to!' I said.

'Don't worry,' she replied cheerfully. 'You'll

still only have to pay half.'

At the top of the hill, at Journey's End, Angie ran up to yank the last drop of truth out of Neville. I didn't run up after her. I sank to the step, gasping for breath. Even from the step I could hear her hammering the door of Flat 1. And shouting.

'Come out, you little horror! Open up! We want words with you!'

I hauled myself up the stairs one knee at a time and collapsed on the halfway platform. Angie was still yelling and hammering. She tried the handle. The door was locked.

'It's no good locking the door! You can't hide forever!'

'How did he…lock the…door?' I wheezed.

'Probably dragged a chair over and climbed on it. I don't care. OPEN UP!' she yelled, half-deafening me.

'Angie!'

This wasn't me. It wasn't Neville. Wasn't even Judy.

'Come away from there!' Audrey said from the top of the stairs.

'We need to talk to him!' Angie shouted. She'd

forgotten to turn off Shout Mode. Also forgotten that her mother didn't know who she meant.

'That's not talking,' Audrey said sternly. 'I won't have you speaking to people that way. Get up here! Now!'

Just before we went up, Angie put her mouth to the door and said, just loud enough for small ears to hear through the wood: 'We've got the triiiiident.'

There was a yelp on the other side, and a rattling sound like a little hand trying to turn a big key, but he'd missed his chance. He'd have to wait till tomorrow. So would Pete.

Chapter Twentythree

'I didn't take this.'

It was just after tea that same evening and Audrey was flipping through the digitals in the little viewscreen on the back of her camera. She'd only taken a few snaps in Wonkton, and none at The Wizard World because she'd left it behind.

'I forgot about that,' Angie said, taking a gander. 'I took it at the wax museum in town earlier.'

'You didn't say anything about going to the wax museum,' Audrey said sharply. She was still miffed with her for the shouting and hammering.

'Didn't I? Well Jig and I went to the wax museum. In town. Earlier.'

'Let's see,' I said.

Angie brought the camera over. 'Doesn't look so much like Pete here,' she said.

She said it very quietly. Didn't want to get the GOs going on the 'imaginary friend' trip again.

'That's because it isn't Pete,' I said. 'And why isn't

it Pete? Because Mr Striker didn't turn him to wax. And why didn't Mr Striker turn him to wax?'

'Because there's no Mr Striker.'

'Exactly. And if Pete isn't all waxy, Neville can't bring him out of it when he gets his trident back. Which means Pete is somewhere else.'

'Out of existence,' said Angie.

'Right. And Nev put him there after all.'

She was still looking at the snap in the back of the camera.

'I can't believe I was so wrong about this. The more I look, the less it looks like him.'

'You wanted to believe it was him,' I said. 'Wanted to believe and you convinced yourself. Should have listened to me. Make a change if you did, but you should have listened.'

She glared at me. 'And I suppose *you* never jump to false conclusions.'

I smiled kindly. 'I've jumped to one or two in my time. But not lately. It's something some of us grow out of. Don't worry about it. You'll get through it. Maybe. If you work really hard at it.'

'Ha!'

She flounced off. She does a great flounce, old

Ange. Wish I could flounce like that. Mind you, people would talk.

Next morning we went into a huddle over the Choco Pops. We had the trident. The one Neville wanted. There couldn't be any doubt this time. We'd tugged it out of the mitt of the happy doll in the wrong suit and looked it over. It wasn't plastic. It was some sort of very light metal, a bit bendy, nothing special. We passed it to one another and back again. We felt nothing. No power. It was just an ordinary toy.

'What if it doesn't work?' I said. 'What if it doesn't do what Neville expects and give him his size back?'

'It's got to.'

'But suppose it doesn't. He's not going to say, "Well, hey, you did your best, you can have Pete back anyway".'

'Mm,' said Angie, like she does when she doesn't have an answer.

To find out if the trident worked, and what he would do if it didn't, we had to get Neville on his own. It was obvious why he'd locked the door against us last night. Keen as he was to get his sweaty little hands on the trident he knew that if we'd gone to the shop we'd rumbled the Striker hoax. He panicked when he heard us on the stairs. He might be a devil, but we were an awful lot bigger than him.

It wasn't raining today, so we guessed the Professor would be operating on the beach later. Angie suggested we go downstairs and offer to help lug his gear and put the booth together. That way we stood more chance of grabbing a few minutes alone with Neville. That's all we needed really. A few minutes to hand the trident over. The reason we didn't do any of this was the mothers, who suddenly announced their plans for the day. Family Plans. Angie and the dads and I immediately started blurting reasons why we'd rather do anything than pay a visit to the tourist farm they had in mind.

'But we haven't done *anything* together yet,' Mum whined.

'We played clock golf with you,' I said.

'Half a round. You got fed up of being beaten and threw your club down.'

'I finished,' Angie said.

'That's because you're not male,' her mother said.

Which made it even worse for us non-female types. We haven't a leg to stand on when they say that sort of thing. Well we have, and more than one as it happens, but we know that we'd better fall in line if we don't want to spend the next three weeks being glared at and not spoken to and having plates slammed down in front of us. Dad and Oliver eyed the blank TV screen sadly like they never expected to see it again, and we all piled into the cars and zoomed off, trying to look happy. At the farm for tourists we joined a million others walking round and round looking at cows and sheep and pigs doing their business in public. We went into a barn and watched cheese being made. We went to the farm shop and looked at corn dollies and jars of honey and fluffy animals and pencil sharpeners and farmy notebooks and jigsaws and postcards and thought we would die of boredom. We went to the steaming hot farm café and bought triangular sandwiches in heavy-duty plastic you needed iron teeth to open, while little kids ran around and babies screamed and kicked and fathers went into trances. Angie and I tried to keep the smiles going because this was a Family Outing, but it wasn't easy, and in the end even the mothers realised it was a pretty feeble way to spend a day of your life. So we went back to Wonkton. In silence.

When we reached Journey's End we all went up to the flat. Ange and I only went for one thing: the trident, which I'd hidden under my bunk with the doll in the devil outfit. The doll stayed put. Him we didn't need.

'Just going for a mooch,' Angie said as we headed for the door.

For once the mothers didn't ask where we were going or tell us to be careful, not talk to anyone and mind traffic. That's because the only people they were talking to was each other. We footed it back down the stairs and the hill and made for the beach and the ex P & J booth. The show was just finishing. The very last show, as it turned out. The Professor had put up a sign saying that this was it, no more, but please come to Striker's Magic Joke Shop (open every day, from tomorrow) where magic and jokes of all kinds could be bought. No one in the audience seemed bothered about it being the last show. The kids sitting in the sand and pebbles got up and charged off almost before the final curtains were drawn.

Ange and I were round the back of the booth when the Prof came out. 'End of an era,' he said when he saw us.

'Sad,' Angie said.

But he didn't look too sad. Kind of relieved, if anything. He was just about to start packing up when his mobile beeped. Text message.

'The rep from my main supplier has arrived,' he said, peering at the screen. 'He wasn't supposed to be here till four.'

'If you have to go, we could mind things till you get back,' Angie said.

'Oh, could you? Could you really? That would be such a help.'

'No prob.'

He poked his head into the booth – probably to tell Neville what was happening so he'd know not to let on that he was alive – and headed up the beach to his van.

'Twenty minutes!' he shouted, walking backwards. 'Half an hour tops!'

'Take your time!'

Time was one thing we didn't waste. We looked

through the flaps. Neville sat hunched up on his box. He seemed nervous.

'Can't hide from us now, can you?' Angie said.

'I told you you'd get your come-uppance,' said Judy, sitting up in her box.

For once he didn't tell her to be quiet. We opened the back of the tent so we could see better.

'Why did you tell us all that rubbish about Mr Striker?' I asked.

Neville raised his hands. 'I couldn't help myself.'

'He can't tell the truth for the life of him,' Judy said.

'That's a lie!' Neville shouted.

'See?' said Judy.

Nev calmed down. He looked kind of embarrassed.

'The old bag isn't entirely wrong,' he said. 'When I was of decent size I could create things people would use or wear which would take the predictability out of their lives and give me a spot of fun. This size, all I can do is baby devil stuff. Turn a budgie into a wasp, a dog into a beetle, bring a ragged old puppet to life, make a kid do back flips or grow fruit and veg...small stuff. Not quality mischief.'

'What's this to do with not telling the truth?' Angie said.

'Comes with the territory. My trap opens and stuff comes out that I have no control over, and then it's too late and it can't be denied.'

'Have you told us *anything* that's true?'

'Sure I have. Well, the odd thing. Being a doll in an attic above the shop and brought to life by lightning, that was true. Dreaming of you three and sensing that you were going on holiday and wanting to get even, that too.'

Then the interrogation began. It doesn't matter who asked which question. This was the first one.

'What about meeting the Professor at the shop when you came back to Wonkton?'

'Partly true. It was him, not Striker, who found me in the shop the night I crept through the cat flap. I'd been caught in a heavy downpour and I was soaked, looking for something to dry myself on when the Prof turned the lights on.'

'Was he more surprised than you said Striker was?'

'Not really. Bit of a gasp, and an "Oh, my lord", but that was it. He's been around puppets all his

317

life. They don't talk to him, but sometimes – he's told me this – sometimes he thinks they might, any minute. I was just proof that it could happen.'

'What did he do?'

'He gave me a nice thick duster to wrap myself in and sat me in front of a little electric fire to warm up. Asked if I wanted a change of clothes because he had some unlive dolls he could borrow from. I said no to the clothes. I like these duds.'

'Didn't he suspect that you were originally one of the dolls?'

'No. And I didn't tell him. I couldn't. I think that's when the lie machine kicked into gear. I told him a story and he believed it.'

'What story?'

'I said I'd been part of a travelling freak show and I'd got lost and they'd gone on without me. He said, "Well, we must try and get you back there," and I said, "Oh no, don't make me go back, the freakmaster is so cruel. He beats me, he starves me, he makes me dance for his friends, let me stay with you." And he did.'

'Nice of him.'

'Yeah. I'd come through the flap at just the right

moment. The Prof was looking for a replacement for Mr Punch, and he asked if I'd be willing to pretend to be a puppet. It was a terrible insult, but he didn't know that, and besides he offered me lodgings at his place plus a small wage.'

'Oh, he pays you then?'

'A *small* wage.'

'Does he know about you bringing Judy to life?'

'No. That was true. He's got enough on his plate without that.'

'Mr Mean's at it again,' said Judy.

'What about the trident?'

'What about it?'

'Did you ask the Professor if you could have it?'

'I couldn't. He didn't know I'd switched togs with the happy moron doll with the side-whiskers. And...'

'And?'

'He was so kind to me.'

'Kind to you? You couldn't ask him for something because he was *kind* to you? That doesn't sound like you.'

He twisted one little leg round the other and stared at the sand.

319

'I can't handle kind. Kind curls my wig. I just cannot ask favours of kind people.'

'We're kind,' said Angie. 'You asked a favour of us. To help you, I mean.'

'That was a demand, not a favour.'

'Followed by blackmail,' I said.

He smiled devilishly. 'There's a lot to be said for blackmail when you want something done.'

'Couldn't you have got the trident back by using your powers?' Angie asked.

'No. To do devilish stuff I have to be in the vicinity. this flat and the beach aren't in the vicinity of the shop.'

'How do we know all this isn't lies too?' I said.

'What do you want, my signature in green blood?' he snapped. 'Listen, my powers are getting smaller by the day. I don't know why – being this size, I guess – but another twenty-four hours and I'll be lucky if I can turn bread and ham into a sandwich. So if you've really got the trident lemme have it and let's end this thing.'

Angie took the trident out of the Striker's Magic Joke Shop bag.

'This it?'

Neville ran out of the booth, reaching for it, fingers twitching eagerly.

'At last! Hand it over!'

She didn't hand it over. She put the trident behind her.

'When we have Pete back.'

Neville's eyebrows came down in a black scowl.

'You don't trust me? Even though I gave you my word to return your pal when I had the trident and devils have to keep their word once it's given?'

'That's right.'

'Well suppose I say forget it, keep the trident. Suppose I say I'll stay like this, it's not such a bad size. You'll be the losers. You'll be the ones who've lost a friend.'

'We have other friends.' This was me.

'Don't give me that. You human kids and your friends. You don't give 'em up just like that. You can't con a conner.'

'OK,' said Angie. 'Let's go.'

She turned away. So did I.

'Wait!' Neville cried. 'OK. Friend first, then trident.'

We turned back.

'Where is he?' Angie asked.

'Stand aside and you'll find out.'

We stood aside.

'I got this from a beachcomber I met a coupla months back,' Neville said. 'Phil...I forget his other name. Something to do with trains. He used a knife, but I found my own way of doing it. A more subtle way. This is the first time I've done it with a human specimen. Interesting to see if he comes out like he went in.'

'Comes out of what?' I said.

'Non-existence. It's just the other side of here.'

He pointed at the empty air.

'There's nothing there.'

'Of course there's nothing there. What do you think non-existence is, tower blocks and bustling shopping centres?'

He reached into a waistcoat pocket and took out something just a bit bigger than his thumbnail.

'What's that?'

'A zip pull.'

'A zip pull without a zip?'

'It's got a zip. I just have to connect it.'

'What to? What for?'

'You'll see. You'll see.'

He hauled one of the puppet boxes out of the booth and climbed onto it. Then he held his arm up as far as he could. There was a little click, as if the zip pull had locked into something, then he pulled downward, slowly, down and down and down, and as he pulled there was a sound like a zip unfastening. A thin gap appeared in the nothingness. There was something in the gap. I looked round it. Behind it. Nothing there, but from the front you could definitely see something. When he'd pulled the invisible zip all the way to the ground Neville stood upright again.

'Neat trick, huh?'

'Did you just do what I think you did?' Angie said.

'If you mean did I fly a camel to Jupiter, no I didn't. If you mean did I unzip reality to let your friend back into existence, you're pretty close to the chalk.'

He stepped aside as we dropped to our knees in front of the gap. Angie touched one edge of it, I touched the other. The edges felt like nothing at all, but they moved when we pulled at them. We tugged them apart. And there, on the other side…

'Pete!'

He was just sitting there, legs crossed, staring ahead of him, not blinking, not seeing, like the waxwork Angie had thought was him but with different eyes, hair, nose and clothes.

'Well, are you going to bring him through before the crowds get here, or just gawp at him?' Neville said.

We pulled the edges of nothing further apart and reached in. Pete still didn't blink. We gripped him by the arms and hauled him through. He toppled over, landed face first on our side of the gap.

'Pull him all the way,' Neville said.

We dragged him nose-down through the sand until he was all the way through. If there'd been time I would have checked what else was on the other side of the gap, but once Pete was clear Neville zipped nothing up again and pocketed the little pull.

'He's been here since Sunday?' Angie asked.

Neville's smile said it all.

'You mean you put him in there while we were helping the Professor?' Neville bowed. 'But didn't he argue? Didn't he resist?'

'Let's just say he fell for my devilish charm.'

'But what's he been doing all this time?'

'Not a lot. When you're removed from existence you don't sit down for regular meals, watch the telly or go dancing.'

Pete was moving now. He was spluttering. Spitting sand.

'Now that he's back,' Angie said, 'will the Golden Old…will our parents remember him?'

'Like he's never been away,' Nev said. 'To them, he'll have been doing whatever you've been doing these past three days.'

'But what about him? What'll Pete remember?'

'Ah, now that's something else again.'

'Who shoved me?' said Pete. 'Who do I have to thump?'

We helped him to his feet.

Chapter Twentyfour

'Well that's my end of the deal,' Neville said. 'Now yours.'

'We'd like some guarantee that you won't make too much mischief once you get your size back,' Angie said.

'Hey, that wasn't in the script. Come on now, I kept my word, you keep yours.'

'But do you really have to be bad?'

'Look,' he said. 'This isn't some feel-good American sitcom where everyone stands round laughing at the end. I'm not Mr Nicey-Nicey. I'm Neville the Devil. With me you don't get raindrops on roses and whiskery kittens. Or copper kettles and warm woolly mittens, for that matter. And you can definitely forget the sleigh bells and doorbells and schnitzel with noodles. Who'd want schnitzel with noodles anyway? You'll get what I give, which'll be fun for one of us if not the rest.'

'I wouldn't give it to him,' Judy said from inside the booth.

'It's not yours to give, beanbag,' Neville said.

'We haven't got much choice,' Angie said to her. She held the trident out. Neville snatched it.

'Finally!'

'What's going on?' said Pete.

We'd only just got him back into existence, but already we'd half forgotten him.

'Don't worry about it,' I said. 'By the way, cool to have you back, Musketeer.'

'Back?' he said. 'What are you talking about? Let's get out of here. The less of see of that little squirt the more I'll like it.'

'Not a little squirt for much longer,' Neville said. 'Pretty big squirt soon. Then you'd better watch how you speak to me. Ah! It's working!'

There he stood, shorter than our knees, hyper as horseradish, gripping the trident with both hands as it started to glow, then…what's the word? Vibrate. Yes, vibrate.

'I knew it!' he said. 'I knew it!'

He looked so devilishly happy. Any minute, any second, he would start to grow. Then he'd be like he was the first time I saw him, a full-sized small man with all the power he needed to make bad mischief.

'Woh,' he said. 'I feel something happening. Am I growing?'

'Not yet,' I said. 'Unless it's starting with your toenails.'

'I feel...'

'What do you feel?' Angie said.

'Power.' He almost whispered it.

'You feel power coming to you from the trident?' I asked.

'No, I...I feel it going out of me.' He sounded puzzled.

'Out of you? That isn't what you expected, is it?'

'No. Not quite.'

'What's the little twit doing?' Pete said.

'Go and build a sandcastle, Pete,' Angie said. 'Be with you in a minute.'

Pete scowled. 'Why doesn't anybody ever tell me anything?'

'It's draining the last of my powers!' Neville said.

'Maybe it has to do that before it can resize you and give you bigger powers,' I said.

'You'd better be right, because if you're not I – eeek!'

He dropped the trident. He'd got some sort of shock from it. He looked at his hands. They were glowing slightly.

'That hurt. It was like it had taken all it wanted, then didn't want to be in my hands any more.' The glow faded. He looked up at us. 'I'm no bigger, am I?'

'Don't seem to be,' Angie said.

'Definitely not,' I said.

'Tee-hee,' said Judy.

'It didn't work! All those months of waiting and planning! All the effort to get you here! All the lies! The humiliation of being Mr Nicey-Nicey! Oh! Oh! Oh!'

'I don't get any of this,' Pete said from somewhere behind us.

'Grrrr,' said another voice. This belonged to a hairy little dog that had run up to stick its nose in our business instead of some other dog's.

'Get away, you brute!' Neville snarled as the dog sniffed him.

The dog didn't get away. It butted Nev's chest with its wet nose. Neville jumped back so sharply that his

329

hat came off. He tweaked one of the little stumps on his head. The stump didn't grow into a horn like he must have expected it to, but still he waved a hand at the dog.

'Snail!' he cried.

'Woof,' said the dog, not turning into a snail.

Neville rubbed his other stump.

'Worm!' he commanded.

'Brrr?' said the dog, not turning into a worm.

'There's nothing left!' Neville howled. 'Nothing! Nothing!'

I shoo'd the dog away.

'Help me out somebody,' said Judy.

Angie helped her out of her box. Judy was all grins as she did a circular tour of Neville.

'No powers left, eh?' she chortled. 'How sad. What will you do with yourself now, little man?'

She poked him in the ribs with a finger. He didn't seem to notice. Didn't call her a name or slap her hand away.

'So the trident didn't work,' I said. We knew it hadn't worked, it was obvious it hadn't worked, but it was good to rub it in.

Neville looked up at me. He was angry and sorry

for himself, both at the same time.

'Go on, laugh at my misfortune.'

'Thanks. Ha-ha-ha.'

'I'm nothing now,' he said. 'I'm as ordinary as you are. About as devilish as a shoe-horn. I bet that makes you very happy, doesn't it?'

'I wouldn't say happy,' I said. 'But I'm starting to wonder who I can invite to the party.'

'Are you sure this won't work a second time?' Angie said.

I glanced at her. So did Neville. So did Judy. She was holding the little bottle of Hiagra.

'Where did that come from?' I said.

'I forgot to take it out of my pocket yesterday.'

'Well put it back. Don't tempt him, he might give it a try. It might work after all.'

'It won't work,' Neville said. 'Nothing'll work.'

'Why not try it just in case?' Angie said.

'Are you *insane*?' I said. 'We've just got Pete back and – '

'What do you mean "got me back"?' said Pete.

' – and Neville's no longer a threat, and you want to help him become one after all?'

'He did keep his end of the bargain,' she said.

'So did we. It's not our fault the trident drained his powers and didn't make him grow.'

'Still,' she said.

'Still nothing. Put it away.'

Neville had flopped on to the sand. His elbows were on his knees and his jaw was in his hands.

'I'm stuck like this,' he wailed. 'All my dreams of being a really mischievous, really cool biggish devil – gone! I'm powerless. Destined to be looked down on forever. No future. No prospects. I can't even be Mr Nicey-Nicey any more. I'll be lucky if I can get a job as a life model for a garden gnome designer.'

'Let's go,' said Pete. 'It's only Sunday and already I'm bored out of my socks. There must be something better to do than hang out with this mini creep.'

'It's not Sunday, Pete,' I said. 'It's Wednesday.'

'Wednesday? What are you on about, McCue? We only arrived yesterday. That was Saturday. Now that you've got the alphabet sorted, you really ought to work on this day of the week thing.'

'No, Pete, it really is We…'

I stopped. As far as he was concerned no time had

passed since his vanishing act. He didn't know he'd vanished and he would take some convincing. Being Pete there would be a lot of argument, a lot of snide remarks about us trying to make a fool of him. We'd get there in the end, somehow – show him the date on a newspaper, get total strangers to back us up in shops, that sort of thing – but it would take work. And when he finally accepted it the moans would start about losing three days of his holiday and how this wouldn't have happened if we'd gone to JoyWorld, and on and on and on he'd go, and me and Ange would start wishing we'd left him out of existence a bit longer. Like ten years.

I noticed that Neville and Angie were talking. She was kneeling in the sand in front of him. She'd taken the top off the bottle of Hiagra and was holding it out to him, trying to get him to give it a go in spite of the small print. He was still refusing, saying it was pointless.

'Leave it, Ange,' I said. The world's better off with him like this.'

'I feel sorry for him,' she said. 'Look at him. So small, so sad. Go on, Nev. Just a splash. Let's see if it – '

333

'I don't want anyone feeling sorry for me!'

Neville smacked Angie's hand in fury. The bottle flew into the air, turning over and over. Some of the liquid spilled out.

'That's it!' Pete said. 'I've had it. You two might like to play with dolls, but I don't. I'm gone.'

'Pete, wait,' I said. But he was off, stomping along the beach.

'Let him go,' Angie said. 'We'll sort him out later.'

'Oh my,' said Judy.

We turned to see what she was oh-mying about.

She was looking at her hand. A hand that a few drops of Hiagra had landed on. A hand that was suddenly quite a bit bigger than usual. Like the rest of her.

'Oh my, oh my, oh my,' she said, as she grew and grew and grew, clothes and all.

'Look what you've done!' Neville cried, hands flying to his cheeks in dismay.

'It's your fault, not mine,' Angie said. 'You knocked my hand.'

Judy stopped growing when she was about our height. This meant that she wasn't a tall woman, but she wasn't a terrifically tiny one any more either. She seemed OK with that. In fact she couldn't get over it.

'Look at me,' she said, turning round and round to show herself off. 'Will you just look at me!'

'All right for some, isn't it?' Neville said.

'All right for me,' Judy said, bending over him.

'But what am I going to do with *you*, little man?'

'You keep away from me.'

She put her hands on her hips and shook her head at him.

'You can't talk to me like that any longer. I'm bigger than you now, ickle sunbeam.'

She bent down and scooped him up in her arms.

'Hey! Whaddayadoin'?'

She didn't say. But when Nev was tucked under her arm she turned to us. She was crazy-happy. Big blue eyes, rosy cheeks, hair like a hedgehog, but as perky as a whistling kettle – unlike Neville, kicking and struggling and unable to do a thing about it.

'I would like to thank you for this,' Judy said, to me as well as Angie. 'I would like to thank you most sincerely.' She spoke differently now. Not quite so much like someone who just climbed out of a haystack.

'Our pleasure,' Angie said, for both of us.

'Put me down, you great bag of wind!' Neville shouted.

'Oh no,' said Judy. 'I have plans for you, little chap.'

He stopped kicking. Looked worried. 'Plans? What plans?'

'I'll tell you as soon as I've made some,' said Judy, and off she went along the beach, Neville kicking and struggling again, under her arm.

'We'll have some explaining to do when the Prof gets back,' Angie said as we watched them go.

'Might have to tell a porkie,' I said. 'Say some yobs came along and swiped them or something.'

'Yes. Hey, you know the trident drained Neville's powers? I wonder if it's still got those powers? I mean, *in* it.'

It lay in the sand where Neville had dropped it. It wasn't glowing any more. Looked like any other toy trident. Harmless.

'You mean if any of the powers it sucked from

Neville would be passed back to some other person holding it?'

'Yes.'

'Better get rid of it just in case,' I said. 'We don't want any more devils around, even in Wonkton-on-Sea, which could do with some livening up. There's a bin over by the ice cream hut.'

Angie nodded. She picked up the trident with a finger and thumb, not really wanting to touch it at all. She blew sand off it and started towards the bin, but stopped after two steps.

'Jig, it's quivering. Feel.'

I added a finger and thumb to hers on the trident. She was right, it was quivering. We were still fingering and thumbing it when it started to glow.

'I have a sudden bad feeling about this,' Angie said.

'Nice to know I'm not the only who gets 'em,' I said.

'I think we ought to let go of it.'

'I'm trying. I can't.'

'No, nor can I. My finger and thumb feel glued to it.'

337

'Do you feel as if something's...flowing into you?' I said.

'Yes. Like when you're downing a hot drink on a cold day.'

'Or a cold drink on a hot day.'

'Mm. And...Holy Christmas!'

Her spare hand shot round the back of her. So did mine. I mean round the back of me. We felt our rear ends. Something was happening back there. Down there. We looked over our shoulders. I couldn't see my rear over my shoulder, but I could see Angie's. Like me, she was wearing jeans, and her sit-upon seams were pulling apart just enough for a red arrow-head to poke out, then poke further out, and further still, until...it became a tail. A devil's tail.

Just like mine.

Chapter Twentyfive

The trident slipped from our fingers and thumbs. It didn't need us to hold on to it any more. It had passed 'essence of devil' to us. We were still staring at one another, rooted to the spot, when the hairy little dog that had bugged Neville ran up. It grabbed the trident in its jaws, and shot off with it. Watching it go gave us something else to look at than one another. Another tail. For ten seconds, maybe twelve, the dog raced along the beach with the trident. But then something happened. In the last few of these ten or twelve seconds the mutt stopped running on sand and started running on air. It still had the trident in its teeth and its feet were still going like the clappers as it scampered towards the nearest cloud.

An airborne dog might have been a sight worth seeing at any other time, but at this time Angie and I had other things to think about. Things closer to home. When we next looked one another in the eye

I knew that she was thinking the same as me. A second later we proved it by saying the same thing at the same instant.

'Hide!'

We spun round. Scooted towards the sea. When we got there we splashed in, knees up, arms out, tails flying. The water must have been cold but we didn't notice. Didn't care.

'What happens when the tide goes out?' Angie said when we were standing in water up to our waists.

'Is this a quiz?' I said.

'No, what happens when the tide goes out?'

'Well, we have a choice. Either stay here or go out with it. Like on a date.'

'Of course, it could be only temporary,' she said.

'What could?'

'The tail thing.'

'True. But it also could be permanent. What then?'

'Dunno. Only one way to find out.'

'What's that?'

'Wait and see.'

So we stood there, half under water, half not,

waiting to see if our tails would disappear or if they were a permanent fixture. It was a long wait. Such a long wait that I'll stop there if you don't mind. I don't mean stop in the sea, I mean stop telling you about it. You must have had enough by now anyway. I know I have. And this is as good a place to finish as any. I mean I'm as close as I can get to the end of the story. This close. What do you say we call it...the tail end?

Jiggy McCue

Turn the page
to find out about
Jiggy McCue's other
wildly wacky
adventures...

Something's after Jiggy McCue!
Something big and angry and invisible.
Something which hisses and flaps and stabs
his bum and generally tries to make
his life a misery. Where did it come from?

Jiggy calls together the Three Musketeers
– One for all and all for lunch! –
and they set out to send the poltergoose
back where it belongs.

Shortlisted for the Blue Peter Book Award

A Jiggy McCue Story

The Killer Underpants

Michael Lawrence

1 84121 713 1   £4.99

The underpants from hell – that's what
Jiggy calls them, and not just because they
look so gross. No, these pants are evil.
And they're in control. Of him. Of his life!
Can Jiggy get to the bottom of his
problem before it's too late?

"...the funniest book I've ever read."
Teen Titles
"Hilarious!"
The *Independent*
Winner of the Stockton Children's
Book of the Year Award

The Toilet of Doom
A Jiggy McCue Story
Michael Lawrence
1 84121 752 2   £4.99

*Feel like your life has gone down the pan?
Well here's your chance to swap it
for a better one!*

When those tempting words appear on the
computer screen, Jiggy McCue just can't
resist. He hits "F for Flush" and... Oh dear.
He really shouldn't have done that. Because
the life he gets in place of his own is a very
embarrassing one – for a boy.

"Fast, furious and full of good humour."
National Literacy Association
"Altogether good fun." *School Librarian*
"Hilarity and confusion." *Teen Titles*

Michael Lawrence

1 84121 756 5   £4.99

Jiggy McCue wants some good
luck for a change.
But instead of luck he gets a genie.
A teenage genie who turns against him.
Then the maggoty dreams start.
Dreams which, with his luck and this genie,
might just come true.

"Will have you squirming with horror and delight!"
Ottakars 8-12 Book of the Month
"Funny, wacky and lively."
cool-reads.co.uk

£4.99

1 84362 344 7

When the new girl in Jiggy's class sneezes
her nose explodes. Runny nose stuff
everywhere. If you look in the runny nose
stuff you can see the future.

Pity the future is always bad.

But the little round creature from the dump
doesn't care. Future Snot is his favourite
meal. He just laps it up!

Jiggy McCue's clothes keep
disappearing – in public. Suddenly,
when there are teachers, friends,
neighbours and total strangers
about, he hasn't a stitch on.

What's causing this? And what can
Jiggy, Pete and Angie do to stop it?

All is revealed in Jiggy's most
embarrassing adventure yet!

orchard Red Apples

Orchard Red Apples are available from all good bookshops,
or can be ordered direct from the publisher:
Orchard Books, PO Box 29, Douglas, IM99 1BQ
Credit card orders please telephone 01624 836000
or fax 01624 837033 or visit our Internet site: www.wattspub.co.uk
or email: bookshop@enterprise.net for details.

To order please quote title, author and ISBN
and your full name and address.
Cheques and postal orders should be made payable to
'Bookpost plc'.
Postage and packing is FREE within the UK
(overseas customers should add £1.00 per book).
Prices and availability are subject to change.